Nate shifted so that his shoulder brushed against hers, and he lowered his mouth closer to her ear.

"Since that kiss we shared under the mistletoe, I haven't been able to go much longer than that without thinking about you. And when I think about that kiss, I remember how good your body felt against mine, and how surprised—and incredibly turned on—I was by the passion of your response."

"You're right," Allison said. "Our memories are different. But considering that we're going to be working closely together, I think it would be best if we both just forgot about that kiss."

"I already know that I can't."

"Maybe you just need to try a little harder."

"Are you saying that you have forgotten?"

"I'm saying that I'm not ⬚⬚⬚⬚⬚⬚⬚ et anything interfere with ⬚⬚⬚⬚⬚⬚⬚⬚⬚⬚ ship."

"I⬚⬚ ⬚⬚⬚⬚⬚⬚⬚⬚⬚⬚⬚ from pleasure," he⬚⬚⬚

"Le⬚⬚ ⬚⬚⬚⬚⬚⬚⬚⬚⬚⬚ss," she suggested.

"Tha⬚⬚ ⬚⬚⬚⬚⬚⬚ like nearly as much fun."

"I like my job and I want to keep my job. Which means I'm definitely not going to sleep with my boss."

His lips curved. "I'm not your boss yet."

Those Engaging Garretts!: The Carolina Cousins

Dear Reader,

Even good girls do, at least once in a while. That's how Allison Caldwell justifies the steamy kiss she shared with her soon-to-be boss, Nathan Garrett. But it was just a kiss! She has absolutely no intention of allowing the attraction between them to go any further...until they're stranded together during an unexpected snowstorm.

Nathan Garrett isn't a forever kind of guy. Even though both of his brothers have recently ventured down the matrimonial path, he has no interest in following their lead. Maybe he's been thinking about his new executive assistant more than he should, but the sexy single mother comes with too many strings—and he has no intention of getting tangled up...

Both Allison and Nathan are about to learn that life sometimes takes interesting and unplanned detours. I hope you enjoy following them on their journey.

Happy Valentine's Day,

Brenda Harlen

PS: Nate's cousin, Ryan, is next in line for his own happily-ever-after. I hope you'll watch for his story—coming soon!

The Daddy Wish

Brenda Harlen

HARLEQUIN® SPECIAL EDITION®

Recycling programs
for this product may
not exist in your area.

ISBN-13: 978-0-373-65867-1

The Daddy Wish

Copyright © 2015 by Brenda Harlen

Printed in U.S.A.

Brenda Harlen is a former attorney who once had the privilege of appearing before the Supreme Court of Canada. The practice of law taught her a lot about the world and reinforced her determination to become a writer—because in fiction, she could promise a happy ending! Now she is an award-winning, national bestselling author of more than thirty titles for Harlequin. You can keep up to date with Brenda on Facebook and Twitter or through her website, brendaharlen.com.

Books by Brenda Harlen

Harlequin Special Edition

Those Engaging Garretts!

A Wife for One Year
The Single Dad's Second Chance
A Very Special Delivery
His Long-Lost Family
From Neighbors...to Newlyweds?

Montana Mavericks: 20 Years in the Saddle!

The Maverick's Thanksgiving Baby

Montana Mavericks: Rust Creek Cowboys

A Maverick under the Mistletoe

Montana Mavericks: Back in the Saddle

The Maverick's Ready-Made Family

Reigning Men

Royal Holiday Bride
Prince Daddy & the Nanny

Visit the Author Profile page at Harlequin.com for more titles.

Writing is often a solitary venture...but not this time! During the writing of much of this book, I was blessed with the company of an incredible group of women, and I would like to dedicate this story to the CBs who were an integral part of the process: CMS, JenB, RSS, GP and Theresa, with an extra special thank you to JenB and "Mr. JenB" for their generosity and hospitality. (xo "35")

This story is also dedicated to Becky with thanks for the tour, the stories, and answers to my endless questions. All the good stuff is hers—any mistakes made or liberties taken are my own.

Prologue

The Garrett Furniture Christmas party was held at the Courtland Hotel in downtown Charisma, as it had been for each of the past six years that Allison Caldwell had worked for the company. The main ballroom was decorated for the occasion with miles of pine garland, dozens of potted evergreens twinkling with lights and white poinsettias at the center of every table. The meal was a traditional roast turkey dinner served family style, with stuffing, mashed potatoes, gravy, buttered corn, baby carrots, green beans and cranberry sauce.

The Garretts always treated their staff well—from holiday parties to summer picnics, from comprehensive benefit packages to generous vacation allowances—and Allison would always be grateful that a three-week temp position had paved the way to her becoming the executive assistant to the CFO. Tonight, she was seated at a table with three coworkers from the finance department and their respective spouses, and throughout the meal, conversation flowed as freely as the wine. No one seemed to notice or care that she was on her own. No one except Allison.

She'd been married once—for all of two minutes. Actually, it had been two and a half years, but that two-and-a-half-year marriage had ended six years earlier. Since the divorce, she'd become accustomed to attending social events on her own, and she usually preferred it that way.

But on this night, only twelve days before Christmas, as

she watched various couples snuggle up to each other in the corners or move together on the dance floor, she was suddenly and painfully aware of her solitary status. Aware that she would be going home to a dark and empty apartment because Dylan was spending the weekend with his dad's new family. Her eight-year-old son was the light of her life, the reason for everything she did, and she missed him unbearably when he was gone.

A surreptitious glance at her watch confirmed that it was almost eleven o'clock—still early for the die-hard partyers but an acceptable time for her to head out. She wished her boss and his wife a merry Christmas, then made her way to the cloakroom to get her coat.

She paused in the wide arched entranceway when she heard voices emanating from within. It took only a few seconds for her to realize there was only one voice—and that it was a familiar one. Nathan Garrett, the CFO's nephew and heir apparent, who would be her boss one day, was talking to someone on the cell phone that was pressed up against his ear. Glancing up, he flashed her the quick, easy smile that never failed to make all of her womanly parts tingle.

All of the Garretts—men, women and children—were beautiful people, and Nathan was no exception. He stood about six-two, with a lean but powerful build that was showcased nicely in formal business attire. His hair was dark, his eyes were an amazing gray that—depending on his mood—looked like smoke or steel, and dimples flashed when he smiled. It was those dimples that got to her, every time.

Not that she'd ever let him know it. Because the man was a major player, and Allison had learned her lesson about players a long time ago.

He disconnected his call and dropped the phone into his jacket pocket.

"I didn't mean to intrude," she said.

"A beautiful woman is never an intrusion," he assured her.

She stepped into the room and began looking for her coat, silently berating herself for the warm flush that colored her cheeks. She didn't respond, because what could she say in response to flirtatious words that came as naturally to him as breathing? And how pathetic was it that she could recognize the fact and still not be able to control the tingle?

"You're not planning to leave already?"

She'd assumed he'd gone and was startled to hear the question, and his voice, so close to her ear.

"It's a great party," she said. "But—"

"So stay and enjoy it," he interrupted.

"I can't. I've got a busy weekend." She told herself that wasn't really a lie, because she did have to get Dylan's Christmas presents wrapped, and that was a task easier done when her son wasn't around.

Finally spotting her coat, she tugged it off its hanger.

"Well, you can't go just yet," he insisted.

"Why not?"

He stepped closer, so close that their bodies were almost touching. She wanted to step back, to give herself space to breathe, but the rack of coats at her back prevented her from doing so.

Nate lifted a hand and gestured to the arched entranceway. "Because you stepped under the mistletoe."

She frowned at the sprig of green leaves and white berries and tried to ignore the wild pounding of her heart inside her chest. "Why would someone put mistletoe in a cloakroom?"

"I have no idea." He crooked a finger beneath her chin to tip her head up. "But tradition demands that a woman passing under mistletoe must be kissed—and I'm a traditional kind of guy."

She couldn't think, she didn't know how to respond to that, and before her brain could scramble to find any words at all, his lips were on hers.

And…oh…wow.

The man definitely knew how to kiss.

Of course, she would have been disappointed to learn otherwise. After all, he had a reputation for seducing women with a word, bringing them to orgasm with a smile and breaking their hearts with a wave goodbye. She'd always assumed those rumors were at least slightly exaggerated, but as his mouth moved over hers, promising all kinds of wicked, sensual pleasures, she was forced to acknowledge that she might have been wrong.

A slow, lazy sweep of his tongue over her lower lip nearly made her whimper. The sensual caress did make her lips part, not just granting him entry but welcoming him inside.

His free hand slid around her back, gently urging her closer. She didn't—couldn't—resist. The coat slipped from her fingers and dropped to her feet, forgotten. There was so much heat coursing through her system, she might never need a coat again. Her hands slid up his chest to his shoulders and she held on, as if he were her anchor in the storm of sensations that battered at her system, pounding self-preservation and common sense into submission.

His tongue danced with hers, a slow and seductive rhythm that teased and enticed. Somewhere in the back of her mind, she knew she should be disappointed to realize that she was no different from any other woman who had succumbed to his charms. But in the moment, in his arms, she really didn't care.

While her body might urge her to let one kiss lead to a mutually satisfying conclusion, she still had enough working brain cells to acknowledge that tangling the sheets with a man who would one day be her boss could be a very big mistake. She eased away from him.

"That's some powerful mistletoe," she said, trying to make light of the intensity of her response.

"I don't think we can blame that on the mistletoe." He bent down to retrieve her coat, then helped her into it. "I'm leaving in the morning to go skiing with some friends, but I'll see you when I get back."

He smiled again, but she ignored the tingles, reminding herself that her job was too important for her to jeopardize for the pleasure of a few hours in his bed. So she only responded with, "My ride should be here by now."

He walked out with her, and she stopped beside the cab that was idling at the curb. "Merry Christmas, Mr. Garrett."

He reached past her for the door handle, but didn't immediately open it. "Don't you think, after that kiss, you could drop the formality and call me Nate?"

No, she couldn't. Because calling him by his given name implied a familiarity she wasn't ready for. "Have a safe trip, Mr. Garrett."

He shook his head, but he was smiling as he opened the door. "I'll talk to you soon, Allison."

She slid into the backseat and gave the driver her address.

He stood on the curb, watching as the cab drove away, but she didn't let herself look back.

Chapter One

Allison wasn't usually the type to spend too much time fussing over her appearance. She never left her apartment looking less than professional—that was a matter of pride—but she didn't usually bother with more than a cursory brush with the mascara wand to darken her fair lashes and a quick swipe of gloss to moisturize her lips.

On the first morning after the holidays, when she found herself digging into her makeup bag for rarely used eye shadow and lipstick, she told herself that she simply wanted a new image for the new year. That the extra care she was taking with her appearance was in no way linked to the possibility that she might cross paths with Nathan Garrett at the office today.

Finally satisfied with the results of her efforts, she poked her head into her son's bedroom. "Come on, Dylan. You don't want to be late on your first day back."

"Yeah, I do," he told her. "School sucks."

She held back a sigh. It worried her that he had such a negative attitude toward school when he was only in third grade, but she'd long ago given up trying to change his opinion and focused her efforts on getting him to class on time. "Okay, but *I* don't want to be late on my first day back."

He eyed her suspiciously. "How come you're all dressed up?"

"What do you mean? I wear this suit to work all the time."

"But you don't wear all that gunk on your face."

She had no ready response to that. If the "slight" improvement she'd been aiming for was obvious enough that her eight-year-old son noticed, she'd definitely gone overboard.

"And your hair's different," he said.

"Go eat your cereal, then brush your teeth," she told him.

It had taken her almost twenty minutes to do her makeup and hair, and less than five to wipe the color off her face and tuck her hair into its usual loose knot at the back of her head.

Dylan didn't comment on the changes, which she interpreted to mean that she now looked as she usually did. She certainly wasn't going to turn any heads when she walked into the office, and maybe that was for the best. Far too many women tripped over themselves trying to catch Nathan Garrett's eye, and she'd always taken pride in the fact that she wasn't one of them.

After dropping her son off at school, she drove across town to the offices of Garrett Furniture, trying not to think about what had happened at the company Christmas party.

Of course, her efforts were futile. It didn't matter that she hadn't seen or heard from Nathan in the twenty-three days that had passed since they'd connected under the mistletoe—she hadn't stopped thinking about him or THE KISS.

Which was ridiculous, because he really wasn't her type. Not that she had a type—she couldn't even remember the last time she'd had a date. But if she *did* have a type, it would *not* be a too rich, too sexy, too good-looking and far too self-assured man who had a reputation for enjoying women of *all* types.

She decided it was a good thing that she'd wiped off her makeup and tied back her hair. The last thing she needed was for Nathan Garrett—or anyone else in the office—to think that she was interested in him.

Maybe her response wasn't about the particular man so much as the fact that she hadn't been kissed (even in lowercase letters) in a very long time. Maybe that was the real reason he'd stirred up desires so long dormant, she hadn't been certain she was capable of feeling them anymore. Maybe she didn't want her boss's nephew so much as she wanted to connect with someone. *Anyone.*

As a single mother, she didn't have time to be lonely—except for every other weekend when Dylan was with his dad, and Dylan had been with his dad the night of the Christmas party. She never would have stayed out so late, or let herself drink so much, if her son had been waiting for her at home. Not that she'd had so much to drink—probably not more than three glasses of wine. But she'd decided that being under the influence of alcohol was a convenient explanation for her uncharacteristic behavior.

And now she was acting like a schoolgirl with a crush on the most popular boy in class—trying to pretty herself up to get his attention. It was pathetic, especially when she wasn't even sure that she liked the guy all that much.

Not that she *dis*liked him.

Allison blew out a frustrated breath. This was ridiculous. *She* was being ridiculous—spending far too much time obsessing over THE KISS and in danger of starting to think about Nathan Garrett as THE MAN. He was simply *a* man—no more and no less. Even if he was a man who could kiss far better than any other man in her experience.

She pulled into her usual parking spot and turned off the ignition. After the holiday, she was eager to get back into the familiar routines of work again, but she stopped by the break room first to grab a cup of coffee. While there, she wished a happy New Year to Melanie Hedley, who was doing the same.

"How was your holiday?" Melanie asked.

"Quiet," Allison said. "Yours?"

"Amazing." The other woman fairly gushed the word. "I went to Vail before Christmas and stayed at this *fabulous*

condo resort that had fireplaces in *every* bedroom and hot tubs on *all* the decks. And Nate and I discovered the most *incredible* little café tucked away in the foothills."

Allison sloshed coffee over the back of her hand and sucked in a sharp breath as the hot liquid scalded her skin. "That does sound…amazing," she said, grabbing a paper napkin to wipe the spilled coffee off her hand.

"Lanie—" Enrico Sanchez poked his head into the room "—we need you on that conference call."

"Oh, right." Melanie smiled at her. "We'll catch up more later."

Allison added a splash of cream to her cup, stirring mechanically while all the excited anticipation that had fueled her buoyant mood only a few minutes earlier fizzled out like air from a balloon.

She wasn't unaware of Nate's reputation, but it still hurt to realize that, only a few days after he'd kissed her, he'd been dining with Melanie in Colorado. It shouldn't. She had no right to be upset or disappointed or anything. He'd certainly never made her any promises, and she wouldn't have believed him if he had.

So why had she let her own imagination paint unrealistic dreams? Why had she ever let herself believe that THE KISS had been anything more than a kiss?

She hated being taken for a fool. Worse, she hated *being* a fool. She sat down at her desk and turned on her computer, determined to put all thoughts of the man from her mind once and for all.

John Garrett walked in while she was still reviewing email messages that had come through over the holidays. He was a good boss and a genuinely wonderful man, and she greeted him with a sincere smile.

The smile froze on her lips when he said, "I'm glad you're here—I need to talk to you about Nathan."

* * *

Allison took her iPad into John Garrett's office.

Though he'd said he wanted to talk to her about Nathan, she didn't think there was any way he could know what had happened at the Christmas party. But HR frowned upon personal relationships in the workplace, and her heart was hammering against her ribs as she perched on the edge of the chair facing his desk.

The CFO looked uncharacteristically burdened and weary. She could practically feel the knots forming in her belly—twisting and tightening—as it occurred to her that she might very well be on the verge of losing her job because she'd had too much to drink and had foolishly and impulsively let herself get caught under the mistletoe by her boss's heir apparent.

"You're no doubt aware that Nathan has been chosen to take over as CFO when I retire," John continued.

She exhaled slowly, reassured by his opening that whatever this was about, it wasn't about the kiss. (The brief exchange with Melanie in the staff room had succeeded in relegating the event to lowercase status.) Her relief was so profound, it took several seconds longer than it should have for the rest of his statement to sink in.

Retirement? Why was he mentioning it now?

"But that's not until June," she noted. And only then if he didn't decide to postpone it again, as he'd done twice already.

"Actually, I'm going to be finished here as of the end of January."

"What? Why?"

"I had a little bit of a health scare over the holidays," he admitted.

She was instantly and sincerely concerned. John Garrett might be her boss, but over the six years that they'd worked together, he'd also become a friend and something of a father figure to her. "What happened? Why didn't anyone call me?"

"It was just a minor blip with my heart—nothing too serious."

The fact that he was sitting behind his desk and not in a hospital bed confirmed that it wasn't too serious, but she knew him well enough to suspect that he was downplaying the "minor" part.

But what did this mean for her? Would she be let go? Was John telling her now as a way of giving her notice that she would be out of a job at the end of the month?

"Nathan's worked hard for the company for a lot of years," he continued. "He's not getting this promotion just because his name is Garrett but because he's earned it."

She nodded, her heart sinking as she considered the repercussions of his announcement. She was confident that she could find another job; she knew John would give her a glowing recommendation. But she wasn't nearly as confident that she would find another job with the comprehensive health-care benefits she needed for the ongoing treatment of her son's asthma.

"That being said, I wanted to be certain that you don't have any concerns about working with him."

"Working with him?" she echoed.

"Is that going to be a problem?"

"No, of course not," she hastily assured him, because she wouldn't let it be a problem. Because he was offering her the chance to keep her job—and her benefits—and she would make it work.

As for the mind-numbing, bone-melting kiss she'd shared with her soon-to-be boss...what kiss?

"I just assumed he'd want to choose his own executive assistant," she said, still not entirely sure Nathan wouldn't do exactly that.

"We've already discussed it," John said. "He wants you."

She knew he only meant that his nephew wanted her to

work for him, but that knowledge didn't prevent her cheeks from flushing in response to his words.

"Now that that's settled, I need you to book a flight to St. Louis for next Thursday," he told her. "There are some minor discrepancies in their numbers that need to be looked at."

Which could probably be done via email, but John had always preferred a hands-on approach.

"Considering the 'minor blip' with your heart, I'm surprised your doctors have given you the okay to fly."

"They haven't," he admitted. "So you'll be going with Nathan."

Allison had to bite her tongue to hold back her instinctive protest as she rose from her chair. It wasn't unusual for John to request that she accompany him on his business trips, but going anywhere with the man who'd kissed her more thoroughly than anyone else in recent memory—maybe ever— filled her with apprehension.

Thankfully, St. Louis was only a two-hour flight from Raleigh, which meant that the trip would be completed in one day. It would be a long day—with a departure at 8:35 a.m. and a return fourteen hours later—but only one day. The trips that the CFO made to review the books of the Gallery stores—more upscale showrooms that carried exclusive, higher-end inventory—located in Austin, Denver, San Francisco, Saint Paul, New York, Philadelphia and Miami, required more time and attention, sometimes necessitating a two or three-night stay.

As Allison returned to her desk, she could only hope that Nathan would decide he didn't need his executive assistant to accompany him on those, because she didn't trust herself to spend that much time in close proximity to the man. Sex had never been casual to her. Even when she was in college, she'd never hooked up with a guy just for a good time. And she'd tried to steer clear of the guys who were reputed to

sleep with different girls every weekend. No doubt, Nathan
Garrett had been one of those guys.

She'd heard rumors of his extracurricular activities, and
while the whispered details might vary, the overall consen-
sus was that the current VP of Finance definitely knew how
to pleasure a woman.

Which was definitely *not* something she should be thinking about right now—especially when the man himself was
standing in front of her desk.

He was the only man she'd ever met who managed to
make her feel all weak-kneed and tongue-tied in his presence. She hadn't worked at Garrett Furniture long before
she'd recognized that the family had won some kind of ge-
netic sweepstakes. The three brothers who ran the company
were of her parents' generation but still undeniably handsome, and all of their children—most of whom were em-
ployed at the company in one capacity or another—were
unbelievably attractive.

It had been an impartial observation—nothing more.
She'd been too busy trying to settle into her new job, put
her life back together and be a good mother to her toddler
son to be attracted to anyone. And then, in her second year
of employment in John Garrett's office, his nephew Nathan
moved back to Charisma.

By then, Allison's wounded heart had healed and her
long-dormant hormones were ready to be awakened again.
And they had jolted to full awareness when Nathan walked
into the office and found her struggling to fix a paper jam
in the photocopier.

He'd come over to help, and just his proximity was
enough to make her skin prickle. When he'd reached around
her, his chest had bumped her shoulder, and the incidental
contact had made her nipples tingle and tighten. He'd dis-
lodged the paper, she'd stammered out a breathless "thank
you" and then he'd gone in to see his uncle.

Four years later, she still wasn't immune to him. She'd learned to hold her own in conversations with him, but she hadn't learned to control her body's involuntary response to his nearness. Even now, even with him standing on the other side of her desk, her blood was pulsing in her veins.

She forced a smile and desperately hoped that her cheeks weren't as red as they felt. "Good morning, Mr. Garrett."

His answering smile didn't seem forced. It was effortless and easy and so potent; she was grateful that she was sitting down because it practically melted her bones. "Good morning, Allison."

She forced herself to glance away, down at the calendar on her desk. "Your uncle is free, if you want to go in."

"I will," he said, but eased a hip onto the edge of her desk. "But first I wanted to apologize for not calling you when I got back from my ski trip."

"Oh, well." She kept her gaze focused on the papers on her desk, because his proximity was wreaking enough havoc on her hormones without looking at him and remembering how his mouth—somehow both soft and strong, and utterly delicious—had mastered hers, or how those wickedly talented hands had moved so smoothly and confidently over her body. "I know the holidays are a busy time for everyone."

"And then Uncle John had his heart attack the day after Christmas." She glanced up and could tell, by the seriousness of his tone and the bleakness in his eyes, that he was still worried about his uncle.

"So it was more than a minor blip," she remarked.

"Is that what he told you?"

She nodded.

"The doctors did say it was minor, but it was definitely a heart attack."

"That must have come as a shock to all of you," she said.

He nodded. "Aside from smoking the occasional cigar,

he didn't have any of the usual risk factors, but the doctors strongly urged him to make some lifestyle changes."

"He's already asked me to look into that cruise he's been promising your aunt for the past few years."

"Retirement is going to be a big adjustment for him, so it will be good for him to have something to look forward to."

"It's going to be a big adjustment for the whole office," Allison agreed.

"And not exactly the adjustment I was hoping to make in our relationship," Nate said.

Our relationship.

She wasn't exactly sure what that was supposed to mean, but her heart gave a funny little jump anyway—before she ruthlessly strapped it down. "Mr. Garrett—"

"Really?" His brows rose and his lips curved in a slow, sexy smile that made her want to melt into a puddle at his feet. "Are you really going to 'Mr. Garrett' me after the—"

"There you are, Nate."

She exhaled gratefully when John poked his head out of his office and interrupted his nephew. Because whatever he'd been about to say, she didn't want to hear it.

Nathan held her gaze for another moment before he turned his attention to his uncle. "I didn't mean to keep you waiting."

"Normally I wouldn't mind," John told him. "But we've got a lot of ground to cover in the next twenty-five days."

Nate nodded. "I'll look forward to catching up with you later," he said to Allison, already moving toward the CFO's office.

She didn't bother to respond, because as far as she was concerned, there wasn't anything to catch up on.

Whatever might have started between her and her soon-to-be boss under the mistletoe was over when he flew off to Vail with Melanie Hedley the next day. And that was for the best. Not only because she didn't want to make a fool of herself—again—where Nathan Garrett was concerned, but because any fantasy she might have had about getting naked with the VP of Finance was inappropriate enough, but the same fantasy with the company CFO could be fatal to her employment.

And that was a risk she wasn't willing to take.

"How was your first day back?" Allison asked when she picked her son up from his after-school program.

Dylan made a face as he buckled up in the backseat.

"Do you have any homework?"

"Yeah. I've gotta write a stupid journal entry about my holiday."

"Why do you think it's stupid?"

"Because it's the same thing Miss Cabrera made us do last year. And because I didn't do anything really exciting. Not like Marcus, who went to Disney World. Or Cassie, who got a puppy."

His tone was matter-of-fact, but she was as disappointed for him as he obviously was. Unfortunately, peak-season trips weren't anywhere in her budget, and pets—especially dogs—weren't allowed by the condominium corporation. "But we had a nice holiday, anyway, didn't we?" she prompted.

"I guess."

"What was your favorite part?" she asked, hoping to help him focus on the highlights.

"Not being at school."

She held back a sigh. Her son's extreme shyness made it difficult for him to make friends, but she didn't understand how he could prefer to be alone playing video games rather than interacting with other kids his own age. At the first parent-teacher meeting of the year, Miss Aberdeen had suggested that he was bored because the work was too easy for him, but when she offered to give him more advanced assignments, Dylan had been appalled by the prospect of being singled out. So he continued to do the same work as his classmates and continued to be bored at school. "What was your favorite part aside from not being at school?" she prompted.

"I had fun at the cartooning class at the art gallery," he finally said.

"So why don't you draw a comic strip about your holiday?"

His brow furrowed as he considered this suggestion. "Do you think that would be okay?"

"I think Miss Aberdeen would love it."

So once they got home, Dylan sat at the table, carefully drawing the boxes for his comic strip while she made spaghetti with meat sauce for dinner. As she stirred the sauce, she kept an eye on her son, pleased by the intense concentration on his face as he worked.

If she'd told him he had to write a paragraph, he would have scribbled the first thing that came to mind and been done with it. But he was obviously having fun with the cartooning, and she was pleased that he didn't just want to draw a comic strip but wanted to draw a good one.

When the outlining was done, he opened his package of colored pencils, and she felt a wave of nostalgia as she remembered when he used to sit at that same table with a box of fat crayons and scribble all over the pictures in a book. He'd been a fan of single-color pictures and would cover the page with blue or green or red or brown, but rarely would he use a variety of colors.

She'd always loved him with her whole heart, but she couldn't deny that there were times when she missed her little boy. The one who would crawl into her lap for a story at bedtime, who looked to her as the authority of all things and whose boo-boos could be made better with a hug and a kiss. He was so independent now—in his thoughts and his actions. Her little boy was growing up, and he didn't need her in all the ways that he used to.

She was proud of the person he was becoming, and more than a little uncertain about her own future. Being a mother had been such a huge part of her identity for so long, she'd almost forgotten that there were other parts. Being with Nathan Garrett made her remember those parts. He made her think and feel and want like a woman, and she wasn't sure that was a good thing.

Chapter Two

Allison was avoiding him.

It was a fact that baffled Nate more than anything, but he couldn't deny it was true.

Over the next few days, their paths continued to cross in the office. But every time he walked past her desk on the way to see his uncle, she seemed to be on the phone. And every time he walked out again, she scurried away from her desk to retrieve something from the printer or the photocopier or to water the plants on the window ledge.

At first he was amused by her obvious efforts to avoid any continuation of the conversation that had been aborted on their first day back after the holiday, but his amusement soon gave way to exasperation. As a Garrett and VP of Finance in the company, he was accustomed to being treated with respect, even deference.

He was not accustomed to being ignored. Especially not by a woman who had been sighing with pleasure in his arms only a few weeks earlier.

She was acting as if the kiss they'd shared had never happened, and maybe she wished it hadn't. But he could still remember the taste of her lips, somehow tangy and sweet and incredibly responsive; he could still remember the heady joy of her slender curves pressed against him; and he could still remember wishing that he didn't have to be on a plane at six fifteen the next morning, because he could think of all kinds of wicked and wonderful things they might do if they spent the night—and maybe several more—together.

For just a minute, maybe two, he'd considered forgetting about the trip with his buddies. Because the warm softness of Allison's body was a hell of a lot more tempting than the promise of fresh powder on the black diamond trails.

But then she'd pulled away. When she looked at him, he saw in her melted chocolate–colored eyes a reflection of the same desire that was churning through his veins, but there was something else there, too. Surprise, which he could definitely relate to, not having expected a minor spark of chemistry to ignite such a blaze of passion, and maybe even a hint of confusion, as if she wasn't quite sure how to respond to what was suddenly between them—yet another emotion he could relate to.

Even after more than three weeks, he couldn't forget about that kiss and he couldn't stop wanting her. And he wasn't prepared to pretend that nothing had happened. Had he taken advantage of the situation? Undoubtedly. But he hadn't taken advantage of *her*. In fact, she'd met him more than halfway.

And when he got out of his Friday afternoon meeting with his uncle, Nate was going to hang around her desk until Allison had no choice but to acknowledge him. Except that it was after six o'clock when he finally left the CFO's office, and she was already gone.

He caught up with his older brother instead.

"Don't you have a wife and a daughter waiting for you at home?" Nate asked, surprised to find him fiddling with design plans on a tablet.

Andrew shook his head. "They've decided that the first Friday of every month is girls' night out. Tonight the plan was for pedicures, dinner and a movie. And they dragged Mom along, too."

"I doubt much dragging was required," Nate commented,

well aware of how much Jane Garrett doted on all of her family—and especially her grandchildren.

"Probably not," his brother allowed. "But since no one's at home, I decided to take the time to polish up the details on the new occasional tables that should hit the market before next Christmas."

"You do realize it's the ninth of January?"

"Product development takes time and attention to detail," Andrew reminded him.

Nate shrugged. "Right now, I'm more interested in dinner. Did you want to grab a burger and a beer at the Bar Down?"

Andrew saved his progress and shut down the tablet.

"So you know why I was working late on a Friday night," Andrew said, when they were settled into a booth and waiting for their food. "But why were you hanging around the office?"

"I had a meeting with Uncle John that went late."

"I imagine you'll have a lot of those meetings over the next few weeks."

Nate nodded. "He's been in charge for a long time— I know it's not going to be easy for him to let go."

Their uncle had been talking, mostly in vague terms, about retirement for a couple of years now. Now Nate would be sitting behind the big desk in the CFO's office by the end of the month. And from behind that desk, he would have a prime view of the CFO's undeniably sexy executive assistant.

"So why don't you seem thrilled that your promotion is coming through sooner than you'd anticipated?"

"I'm happy about the promotion," Nate said. "I just wish it wasn't happening for the reasons it is." Although he'd frequently lamented the fact that his uncle kept pushing back his retirement, he never wanted it to be forced upon him.

"Now he can finally take Aunt Ellen on that cruise he's been promising since their fortieth anniversary."

"How long ago was that?"

"Almost four years." Andrew sipped his beer. "But somehow I don't think you're thinking about their vacation plans."

"I was just wondering why Uncle John was so insistent that Allison Caldwell stay on as my executive assistant."

"Probably because she's been doing the job for more than six years and knows the ins and outs of the office better than anyone else," his brother pointed out. "Do you have a problem with Allison?"

"No," he said quickly.

Maybe too quickly.

His brother's eyes narrowed. "Tell me you haven't slept with her."

"I haven't slept with her." Nate thanked the waitress who set his plate in front of him and immediately picked up his burger, grateful for the interruption as much as the food.

"Keep it that way," Andrew advised when the server was gone. "She's a valuable employee of the company."

"I'm aware of the code of conduct in the employee handbook," Nate reminded his brother. "I helped write it."

"Along with Sabrina Barton from Human Resources."

Nate bit into his burger.

"Tell me," Andrew said, dipping his spoon into his Guinness stew. "Did you sleep with her before or after the handbook went to the printer?"

"It was a brief fling more than three years ago, *after* she gave notice that she was leaving the company," he pointed out. "And *she* threw herself at *me*."

"The curse of being a Garrett," his brother acknowledged sarcastically. "But you could exercise some discretion and not catch every woman who throws herself at you."

"It's basic supply and demand—and with the number of single Garrett men rapidly dwindling, the unmarried ones are in greater demand." And he very much enjoyed being in demand.

Andrew shook his head as he scooped up more stew. Nate focused on his own plate, and conversation shifted to the hockey game playing out on the wide TV screen over the bar.

The waitress had cleared their empty plates and offered refills of their drinks. They both opted for coffee.

Andrew's cup was halfway to his lips when his cell phone chimed. He read the message on the display, then looked up.

"Problem?" Nate asked.

His brother glanced past him and smiled. "Not at all."

Over his shoulder, Nate saw that Andrew wasn't looking at something but some*one*. Rachel Ellis—now Rachel Garrett—his wife of four months.

She slid onto the bench seat beside her husband and brushed her lips over his. "Hi," she said, her tone soft and intimate.

"Hi, yourself," he said. "How was girls' night?"

"Fabulous." She snuggled close. "We got our toenails painted, then had dinner at Valentino's—with triple-chocolate truffle cake for dessert. But there weren't any good movies playing, so Maura went to your parents' house for a sleepover."

Andrew gestured for the waitress to bring the bill.

Nate sighed. "Whatever happened to bros before—" he caught Rachel's narrowed gaze and chose his words carefully "—sisters-in-law?"

"I'd say sorry, bro, but I'm not," Andrew told him.

"I know you're not."

And Nate *was* happy for his brother. Before he met Rachel, Andrew had spent a lot of years grieving the loss of his first wife and trying to raise his daughter on his own. With Rachel, Andrew and Maura were a family again.

"Why are you hanging out with your brother tonight instead of seducing a beautiful woman?" Rachel asked him.

"I've given up any hope of finding a woman as beautiful as you," Nate replied smoothly.

"Which is the same thing you'd say if Kenna was here instead of me," Rachel guessed.

"Because both of my brothers have impeccable taste."

Andrew signed the credit card receipt and tucked his card back into his wallet.

"What happened to the girl you were with at the Christmas party?"

The mischievous glint in his sister-in-law's eyes made him suspect that she wasn't just fishing for information but had actually seen something that night. "I wasn't with anyone."

"I know you didn't take a date," Rachel acknowledged. "But I definitely saw you come out of the cloakroom with someone."

Nate sipped his coffee and pretended not to know who she was talking about.

Huffing out a breath, she turned to Andrew. "You must have seen her. Pretty blonde in a green dress."

"Sorry," he said. "I didn't notice anyone but you."

"That's so sappy," she said, but she was smiling.

"And true," her husband assured her.

Nate rolled his eyes. "Don't you guys have an empty house waiting for you?"

"As a matter of fact," Andrew said.

"He's changing the subject," Rachel pointed out. "Because he doesn't want you to figure out who she was."

"I didn't leave with anyone that night," Nate said. "I had a six a.m. flight the next morning."

"I didn't say you left with her," she said. "Just that you were in the cloakroom with her."

"Maybe we both went to get our coats at the same time?" he suggested.

Rachel shook her head, unconvinced, but she let her husband nudge her out of the booth. "If your memory clears, you should bring her to dinner Sunday night."

Nate knew that wasn't going to happen. Stealing a kiss from a coworker at the company Christmas party was one thing—inviting his executive assistant to his parents' house to meet the family was something else entirely.

Friday nights always loomed long and empty ahead of Allison after she gave Dylan a hug and a kiss goodbye and sent him off to his dad's house for the weekend.

She tried not to resent the fact that Jefferson and his new wife had a three-bedroom raised ranch on a cute little court in Charisma's Westdale neighborhood. She'd always wanted her son to have a backyard in which he could run and play, and now he did. She just wished it was something she'd been able to give to him every day and not every other weekend when he was with his father.

But she was grateful that they had a nice two-bedroom apartment on the fifth floor of a well-maintained building with a park across the street. The rent wasn't cheap, but after she paid the bills each month, she was able to put aside a small amount of money into a vacation fund. Last summer, they'd gone to Washington, DC. This year, she intended to take him camping—to give her city boy a taste of the outdoors. She had some concerns as to whether or not he'd be able to survive a whole week without television or video games, but she wanted to try.

However, it was only January now, which meant she didn't have to determine their summer plans just yet. In the interim, she should cherish this time on her own: forty-eight hours in which to do whatever she wanted. She could lounge around in her pj's and eat popcorn for dinner while she watched TV if she wanted. She didn't have to prepare meals for anyone else or pick up dirty socks that missed the hamper in the bathroom or pull up the covers on a bed that had been left unmade.

But the sad reality was that she had no life outside of

work and her son. She could go to the bookstore and lose herself in a good story for a few hours, but lately even her favorite romance novels had left her feeling more depressed than inspired.

She wanted to believe in love and happy-ever-after, but real life hadn't given her much hope in that direction. And if she let herself give in to her desire for Nathan Garrett, she was more likely to end up unemployed than marrying the boss, and she had no intention of jeopardizing her job for a hot fling with a man who probably wouldn't remember her name the next day.

Instead, she called her friend Chelsea, thinking that they might be able to catch a movie. As it turned out, her friend was working, but she convinced Allison to come in to the Bar Down for a bite to eat. The sports bar was usually hopping on weekends, so she didn't think they'd have much time to talk, but her growling stomach and the promise of spinach dip were a stronger lure even than her friend's company.

To her surprise, there were only a handful of tables in use, and more of the seats at the bar were vacant than occupied.

"I don't think I've ever seen it so quiet in here on a Friday night," Allison remarked.

Chelsea set a glass of pinot noir on a paper coaster in front of her friend. "It might pick up a little bit later, but the first weekend after the holidays is always slow. Most people are dragging after their first week back at work—or too worried about paying their credit card bills—to want to go out."

"I can understand that," Allison acknowledged.

"And I'm guessing the only reason you're here is that it's Dylan's weekend with his dad."

"Yeah," she admitted. "I've got a thousand things to do at home—with a thousand loads of laundry being at the top of the list—but it just felt too quiet tonight."

"Did you come in here to see me or in search of some male companionship?"

Allison's eye roll was the only response she was going to give to that question.

Her friend sighed. "When was the last time you went out on a date—the night Dylan was conceived?"

"I date," she said.

Chelsea's brows lifted.

"I do. I even let you set me up on that blind date with your cousin Ivan not too long ago."

"Evan," her friend corrected. "And that was more than three years ago."

"It was not."

"It was," Chelsea insisted. "Because he didn't meet Wendy until a few months after that, and they just celebrated their second wedding anniversary."

"Oh." She picked up her glass, sipped. "It really didn't seem like it was that long ago."

"You're a fabulous mother, but you're also a young and sexy woman hiding behind your responsibilities to your son. There should be more to your life."

"I don't have time for anything more."

"You have to make time," her friend insisted. "To get out and meet new people."

"Why can't I just hang out with the people I already know?"

Chelsea sighed. "How long has it been since you've had sex? No—" She shook her head. "Forget that. How long has it been since you've even kissed a guy?"

Sex was, admittedly, a distant and foggy memory. But every detail of that kiss under the mistletoe was still seared into her brain despite all of her efforts to forget about it, tempting her with the unspoken promise of so much more.

"Oh. My. God."

She blinked. "What?"

"You've been holding out on me."

"What are you talking about?"

"I mentioned the word *kiss* and your eyes got this totally dreamy look and your cheeks actually flushed."

Allison's cheeks burned hotter. "It really wasn't that big of a deal."

"I'll be the judge of that," her friend decided. "When? Where? And who?"

Because she knew Chelsea wouldn't be dissuaded, she answered her questions in order. "Before Christmas, at a party. It was just one kiss, and no way am I telling you who."

"*Before* Christmas? And I'm only hearing about this *now*?"

"It wasn't a big deal." Which was a big fat lie, but she mentally crossed her fingers in the hope that her friend might believe it.

"Just one kiss?"

She nodded.

"Honey, if you're still blushing over one kiss more than three weeks later, it isn't just a big deal, it must have been one helluva kiss."

"I haven't been kissed like that in…" Allison tried to think back to a time when another man had touched her the way Nathan had touched her, kissed her as if he wanted nothing more than to go on kissing her, and her mind came up blank "…ever."

"Ty—" Chelsea called out to the man working the other end of the bar. "Can you cover for me for a few minutes?"

He winked at her. "Your wish is my command."

Chelsea rolled her eyes as she came around to the other side of the bar and slid onto the empty stool beside her friend, so they could talk without their conversation being overheard.

"Tell me about your holidays," Allison suggested, hoping to redirect her friend's focus.

Chelsea shook her head. "Uh-uh. This is about *you*, not me."

"But your life is so much interesting."

"Not this time."

Allison traced the base of her wineglass with a fingertip. "It really was just one kiss, and it's not going any further than that."

"Why not?" her friend demanded.

"Because it was the office Christmas party."

"It was someone you work with?"

She nodded.

"How closely?"

"Does it matter?"

"Of course it matters."

"Too closely."

Chelsea sighed. "Can't you give me at least a hint?"

She wished she could. In fact, she wished she could tell her friend everything. But Chelsea was a die-hard romantic, and the last thing Allison wanted or needed was any encouragement. Because even knowing all of the reasons that getting involved with Nathan Garrett would be a mistake, even knowing he'd been with Melanie Hedley in Colorado, she couldn't help wishing he would kiss her again.

"No, because you'll encourage me to do something crazy, and anything more than that one kiss would be totally crazy."

"He really has you flustered," Chelsea mused.

"It looks like Ty could use a hand behind the bar."

"He's fine." Then her attention shifted, and her lips curved. "Although maybe I should vacate this stool for a customer—because there's one headed in this direction who should be able to make you forget the mystery kisser and probably your own name."

Allison turned her head to follow her friend's gaze and sucked in a breath when her eyes locked with Nathan Garrett's cool gray ones.

She immediately turned back to Chelsea. "Are you crazy? He's practically my boss."

She didn't know if it was the words or the heat that she could feel infusing her cheeks, but somehow her response magically tied all of the loose threads together for her friend.

"It was *him*," Chelsea stated. "You kissed Nathan Garrett."

"*He* kissed *me*," she clarified. "And it was only because of the mistletoe."

"If he'd kissed me, I wouldn't have let it end there."

"You mean he hasn't kissed you?"

Her friend's brows lifted. "I know he has a reputation, but it isn't all bad. In fact—" she grinned "—most of it is *very* good. And if he's half as good a kisser as his brother Daniel, I can understand why your pulse is still racing."

"My pulse isn't still racing," she denied.

Chelsea just smiled, rising from her stool as the soon-to-be CFO slid onto the vacant seat on Allison's opposite side.

"What can I get for you, Nate?" Chelsea asked, returning to her position behind the bar.

"I'll have a Pepsi."

"Straight up or on the rocks?"

He smiled. "On the rocks."

The bartender stepped away to pour his soda, and Nate turned to Allison. "You skipped out early today."

She shook her head. "I only take a half-hour lunch each day so I can finish at four on Fridays."

"I wasn't aware of that."

"Is that going to be a problem, Mr. Garrett?"

"I don't see why it would."

Allison picked up her wine, set it down again. Dammit—Chelsea was right. Her pulse was racing and her knees were weak, and there was no way she could sit here beside him, sharing a drink and conversation and not think about the fact that her tongue had tangled with his.

"I think I'm going to call it a night."

"You haven't finished your wine," he pointed out.

"I'm not much of a drinker."

"Stay," he said.

She lifted her brows. "I don't take orders from you out-side of the office, Mr. Garrett."

"Sorry—your insistence on calling me 'Mr. Garrett' made me forget that we weren't at the office," he told her. "Please, will you keep me company for a little while?"

"I'm sure there are any number of other women here who will happily keep you company when I'm gone."

"I don't want anyone else's company," he told her.

"Mr. Garrett—"

"Nate."

She sighed. "Why?"

"Because it's my name."

"I meant, why do you want my company?"

"Because I like you," he said simply.

"You don't even know me."

His gaze skimmed down to her mouth, lingered, and she knew he was thinking about the kiss they'd shared. The kiss she hadn't been able to stop thinking about.

"So give me a chance to get to know you," he suggested.

"You'll have that chance when you're in the CFO's of-fice."

She frowned at the plate of pita bread and spinach dip that Chelsea slid onto the bar in front of her. "I didn't order this."

"But you want it," her friend said, and the wink that fol-lowed suggested she was referring to more than the appe-tizer.

"Actually, I want my bill. It's getting late and…" But her friend had already turned away.

She was tempted to walk out and leave Chelsea to pick up the tab, but the small salad she'd made for her own din-ner after Dylan had gone was a distant memory and she had no willpower when it came to the Bar Down's three-cheese spinach dip.

Allison blew out a breath and picked up a grilled pita triangle. "The service here sucks."

"I've always found that the company of a beautiful woman makes up for many deficiencies."

It was, she was sure, just one of a thousand similar lines that tripped easily off of his tongue. And while she wanted to believe that she was immune to such an obvious flirtatious ploy, the heat pulsing through her veins proved otherwise.

Then he smiled—that slow, sexy smile that never failed to make her skin tingle. It had been a long time since she'd been an active participant in the games men and women played—so long, in fact, that she wasn't sure she even knew the rules anymore.

What she did know was that Nathan Garrett was way out of her league.

Chapter Three

Nate didn't usually have any trouble reading a woman's signals, but while Allison's words were denying any interest, the visible racing of her pulse beneath her ear said something completely different.

She didn't want to want him, but she did. That wasn't arrogance but fact, and one that was supported by the memory of the kiss they'd shared. A kiss that, for some inexplicable reason, she was pretending had never happened. He was tempted to ask her why, but he decided it wasn't the time or the place. Because he knew if he pushed, she'd just walk away—and he didn't want her to walk away.

So he picked up his glass and gestured to the plate in front of her. "Are you going to share that?"

She took her time chewing, as if thinking about his request. Then she shrugged and nudged the plate so that it was between them.

He'd eaten dinner with his brother, but she didn't know that, so he selected a piece of bread and dunked it. He was usually a meat-and-potatoes kind of guy, but the grilled bread in the warm cheesy spinach dip was surprisingly tasty. "This is good," he said.

"And addictive," Allison agreed, popping another piece into her mouth. "Which is why I rarely come here."

"Not because of the poor service?"

Her lips curved, just a little. "That, too."

Her smile, reluctant though it was, stirred something low in his belly.

She was pretty in a girl-next-door kind of way, her sexiness tempered by sweet. Definitely attractive, just not his type. Or so he'd always thought. He'd had countless conversations with her, sat in numerous meetings beside her, and never felt anything more than mild interest.

Until the Christmas party.

When Allison walked into the ballroom that night, it was as if a switch had flicked inside him, causing awareness to course through his blood like a high-voltage electrical current. And he didn't even know why. Sure, she looked different—but not drastically different.

Her hair, always tied in a knot at the back of her head at the office, was similarly styled, but the effect was softer somehow, with a few strands escaping to frame her face, emphasizing her delicate bone structure and creamy skin. Her eyes seemed bigger and darker, and her lips were glossy and pink, and deliciously tempting.

He wasn't sure if he'd ever seen her in a dress before. Certainly he'd never seen her in a dark green off-the-shoulder style that hugged her slender torso and flared out into a flirty little skirt that skimmed a few inches above her knees. Or in three-inch heels that emphasized shapely legs and actually made his mouth water.

She sat with a group of coworkers from the finance department for the meal, and he found himself sneaking glances in her direction—trying to figure out why he was so suddenly and inexplicably captivated by a woman he'd known for four years. He saw her dancing a couple of times early in the evening. She seemed to be pretty tight with Skylar Lockwood, his cousin's office administrator, and they looked to be enjoying themselves. The music was mostly fast and upbeat, with the occasional slow song thrown in to give the dancers a chance to catch their collective breath.

During one of those times, he watched his dad lead his mom to the dance floor. Even after more than forty years of marriage, they had eyes only for each other, and the obvious closeness and affection between them warmed something inside him. He'd never wanted what they had—and what each of his brothers had found with their respective spouses. And yet, he'd recently found himself considering that he *might* be ready for something more than the admittedly shallow relationships that had been the norm in his life for so long. Not that he was looking to put a ring on any woman's finger, but maybe a toothbrush in her bathroom wouldn't be so bad.

The vibration of his phone against his hip had him moving out of the ballroom to respond to the call. The name on the display gave him pause. Mallory was definitely not a woman with whom he would ever have something more, although there had been a time when he'd believed otherwise. Then he'd found out that his flight attendant girlfriend had also been dating a pilot she worked with, an Australian entrepreneur and a French banker during the time they were together.

More than a year after their final breakup, he had to wonder why she was reaching out to him now. And because he was curious, he answered the call. The connection wasn't great, so he moved into the cloakroom—where it was a little bit quieter and more private—to talk to her. While her claims of missing him had soothed his bruised ego, he wasn't at all tempted by her explicit offer to reconnect when she passed through town again.

He'd just tucked the phone back into his pocket when Allison had come in to get her coat. And in that moment, he completely forgot about Mallory and every other woman he'd ever dated. In that moment, he wanted only Allison.

And when he noticed that someone had pinned a sprig of

mistletoe in the center of the arched entranceway, he couldn't resist using it to his advantage.

"Refill?"

The question jarred him back to the present. He glanced up at Chelsea, who was pointing to his empty glass.

"Sure."

The bartender nodded, then shifted her attention to Allison. "One more?"

She shook her head. "No, I'm going to head home."

"Alone?"

"Yes, alone," she said firmly, definitively.

"But it's late," Chelsea protested, looking pointedly in Nate's direction.

"I live down the street," Allison reminded her.

"Down a dark street."

She shook her head. "Could I have my bill, please?"

Her friend looked at Nate again before she moved to the cash register to calculate the tab.

He knew how to take a hint—and he appreciated the opportunity the bartender had given to him. "I can give you a lift home," he told Allison.

"I really do live just down the street—it's not even far enough to drive."

"Then I'll walk with you," he said.

"I appreciate the offer," she said. "But it's not necessary."

"Chelsea thinks it is."

"I don't think that's what Chelsea's thinking," she admitted to him.

His brows lifted at that; Allison just shook her head.

When Chelsea returned with the bill, Nate passed her his credit card. "Add my drink and put it on that."

"I can pay my own bill," Allison protested, but her friend had already walked away again.

"You shared your spinach dip with me," Nate reminded her.

"I wouldn't have eaten the whole thing by myself—or

shouldn't have, anyway." But when he signed his name to the credit card receipt Chelsea put in front of him, she accepted that it was an argument that she wasn't going to win. "Thank you, Mr. Garrett."

"Nate," he reminded her.

She slid off of her stool and picked up her coat. He rose to his feet, intending to walk her to her door.

"I'm just going to the ladies' room," she told him.

"Oh." He sat down again, and watched out of the corner of his eye as she headed toward the alcove with the restrooms.

Chelsea finished serving another patron at the bar, then came back to him, shaking her head. "You're too accustomed to women falling at your feet, aren't you?"

He frowned. "What are you talking about?"

"I'm talking about the fact that you just let Allison slip out the door."

"She just went to the ladies' room."

"With her coat?"

He swore under his breath as he reached for his own.

Chelsea put her hand on his arm, shaking her head. "If you chase after her now, you're not only going to look pathetic, you're going to scare her away."

He scowled at that.

"I thought you'd appreciate the opportunity to walk her home," she continued. "But maybe you're not as interested as I thought."

"Just because you once dated my brother for a few weeks doesn't give you the right to pry into my personal life."

"No," she agreed. "But the fact that I'm Allison's best friend gives me the right to pry into hers."

"Then why aren't you talking to her?"

"I tried," she admitted. "But she doesn't kiss and tell."

However, the twinkle in her eye in conjunction with her word choice suggested that she knew more than she was letting on.

"Neither do I," he said.

"So don't talk," she said. "Just listen."

He picked up his soda and sipped.

"She doesn't date—or hardly ever, and she definitely doesn't sleep around. So if you're not looking for anything more than a good time, you should look elsewhere."

"I don't know what I'm looking for," he admitted.

"Then you better figure it out. And if you decide you want Allison, be prepared for the obstacles she'll put in your path every step of the way."

"Is that supposed to be a challenge or a warning?"

"That depends entirely on you," Chelsea said.

Nate considered what she'd said as he walked out of the bar. She was right—he could take her words as a warning and decide to forget about the sexy executive assistant, and that was probably the smart thing to do. On the other hand, he was more intrigued by Allison Caldwell than he'd been by any other woman in a very long time—and he never turned away from a challenge.

"Come on, Dylan. Your breakfast is on the table."

It was the third time she'd called to him, and finally he wandered out of his bedroom, still in his pajamas, his hair sticking up in various directions. She looked at her sleepy-eyed son and felt the familiar rush of affection.

She hadn't thought too much about getting married or having a baby before she found herself pregnant at twenty-one, but she'd never believed her son was anything but a gift. He wasn't always an easy child—there were times when he challenged and frustrated and infuriated her, but she loved him with every ounce of her being.

As he passed her on the way to the table, she gave him a quick hug and dropped a kiss on the top of his head. "Good morning."

"Mornin'," was his sleepy reply. He settled into his usual

chair at the table and scowled at the box of cereal on the table. "Can't I have waffles?"

"Not this morning," she told him.

His scowl deepened as he poured the Fruity O's into his bowl, then added milk. "Can I have pizza in my lunch?"

"We don't have any pizza." She cut the sandwich she'd made in half diagonally and put it in a snap-lock container.

He responded with something that sounded like, "Idon'wannasan'ich," but the words were garbled through a mouthful of cereal.

"It's ham and cheese," she told him. "Your favorite."

"M'favrit'spza."

"Don't talk with your mouth full."

He swallowed. "My favorite's pizza."

"We don't have any pizza," she said again, adding grapes and cookies to his lunch box.

"Can we have pizza for dinner?"

"You're going to be at your dad's for dinner," she reminded him.

He shoveled another spoonful of cereal into his mouth. "I'sThursdy."

"Yes, it is."

"Joslynsgot—"

"Chew and swallow, please."

He did so. "Jocelyn's got piano and Jillian's got dance."

"Lucky for them."

"Not for me," he grumbled. "'Cause I get dragged everywhere with them."

She wasn't without sympathy. She could only imagine how painful it was for an almost-nine-year-old boy to sit around while his younger sisters were involved in their own activities.

"Take your 3DS," she suggested, expecting him to jump at the offer.

"We're not s'posed to have 'lectronics at school," he told her.

She held back a sigh as she zipped up his lunch box and slid it into the front pocket of his backpack, double-checking to ensure that his rescue inhaler was where it was supposed to be. "Keep it in your locker."

He shoved more Fruity O's into his mouth, but he chewed and swallowed before speaking again. "Where's St. Louis, anyway?"

She opened the atlas she kept on hand to assist with his geography homework and pointed out Missouri. "Right there."

He studied the map. "It's a lot farther than Washington."

She knew he meant Washington, DC, which they'd visited the previous summer. "Yes, it is," she confirmed.

"Why do you hafta go there?"

"It's a business trip," she said, trying not to sound impatient as she glanced—again—at the clock.

"When are you gonna be home?"

"Tonight," she said. "And I'll pick you up straight from the airport."

"Promise?"

"I promise."

He pushed back his chair and started to carry his empty bowl and juice cup to the dishwasher. She was trying to teach him to pick up after himself—an uphill battle, to be sure—but she decided that today wasn't a day for lessons. Not if she wanted to get Dylan to school and herself to the airport on time.

"I'll do that." She took the dishes from him. "You go brush your teeth and get dressed."

Thankfully, he didn't drag his heels too much while doing so, and they were only three minutes behind schedule when they walked out the door. If the traffic lights cooperated, she might be able to make up that time on the way. But before Dylan climbed into the backseat of her car, she took the time to give him a hug and a kiss, because she knew he wouldn't accept any outward displays of affection when she dropped him off in front of the school.

He didn't say too much on the drive, and she knew that his mind was already shifting its focus to the day ahead. She was pleased that he did well in school, and frustrated by the realization that his success hadn't led to enjoyment. She thought he might like it more—or at least hate it less—if he made some friends, but he didn't choose to interact with many of the other students, except if the teacher forced them to work in groups, and even then, he didn't say much as he quietly did the work that was assigned.

She pulled up in front of the school as the bell rang and watched as he walked up the front steps to the main doors. It seemed like only yesterday that he'd refused to let go of her hand on his first day in kindergarten. The years had gone so fast, and so much had changed since then. Now he was in third grade, and she was lucky if he bothered to wave goodbye when she dropped him off.

He did today, lifting his hand as he glanced over his shoulder before he pulled open the door and disappeared inside, and the casual gesture tugged at her heart.

Then she pulled away from the school and turned toward the airport.

The acting CFO was already at the gate when Allison arrived.

Nate offered her a smile and a large coffee. "Cream only."

She didn't ask how he knew, she just accepted it gratefully. "Thanks."

As she sipped her coffee, she tried to focus on what she'd told her son—that this was a business trip, not unlike so many other business trips she'd made with John Garrett in the past. Except that this time she was traveling with her boss's nephew, and the memory of that one stolen kiss was still far too vivid in her mind.

When they boarded the plane, she was grateful that flying business class meant they wouldn't be sitting as close together as they would if they were in coach. Although Nathan didn't have the same girth across his belly as his uncle, he was a couple inches taller, his shoulders were broader and his legs were longer.

He paused at the aisle to let her precede him.

"You don't want the window seat?"

"No, I like the aisle."

"Oh. Okay." She slipped past him and into her seat.

He settled beside her and buckled his belt.

His choice of aisle over window wasn't a big deal, except that she couldn't help feeling as if she was trapped between the wall and Nate's body. Nate's long, lean and delicious-smelling body.

She tried to ignore his proximity, but every time she drew in a breath, she inhaled his scent and felt a little quiver low in her belly.

Seriously, the man was dangerous to her peace of mind.

While everyone else was boarding, she kept her attention focused on her tablet, checking her calendar for the dates and times of meetings in the next couple of weeks. Nate, she noted, was reading a newspaper, but he tucked it away when the flight attendant began to review the safety procedures of the aircraft.

Most of the passengers in business class were frequent fliers who probably knew the spiel as well as the staff, and she didn't doubt that he was one of them, but he gave the flight attendant his attention anyway. Or maybe it had nothing to do with the safety procedures and everything to do with her big…smile.

When the presentation was finished, he turned to Allison. "Are we being picked up at the airport?"

She shook her head. "John always preferred to have a rental car rather than be at the mercy of someone else's schedule. I didn't think to ask what arrangements you wanted made."

"I would have told you to make the usual arrangements," he said, and smiled.

And damn if that smile didn't make her toes want to curl.

In an effort to refocus her thoughts, she said, "Did you want to review any of your uncle's notes before the meeting?"

"I did that last night."

"Do you have any questions?"

He shifted in his seat, so that he was facing her more fully. "As a matter of fact, I do."

"Okay."

"Why are you pretending that nothing happened at the Christmas party?"

She felt color climb up her neck and into her cheeks. So much for her determination to stay focused on business. "I meant—do you have any questions about the meeting?"

"No," he said. "But I want to know why you're pretending the kiss we shared never happened."

Since he obviously wasn't going to let her ignore his question, she decided to answer it succinctly and dismissively. "Not making a big deal out of it isn't the same as pretending it never happened."

"So you do remember it?"

She scrolled through the notes on her tablet. "I remember that it was late, there was mistletoe, we both had a little too much to drink and got caught up in the spirit of the holiday."

"Do you want to know how I remember it?"

"I'm actually a little surprised that you do."

"What is that supposed to mean?"

"I would have thought your sojourn with Melanie would

have eradicated one meaningless little kiss from your mind," she said.

"Let's put aside the inaccuracy of your description until after you explain who the hell Melanie is."

"Melanie Hedley," she said.

"The name sounds vaguely familiar," he admitted.

"Perky blonde, works in marketing."

His confusion finally cleared. "You mean Lanie?"

"Yeah, I guess I have heard some people call her Lanie."

"And the sojourn?" he prompted.

"Your ski trip."

He shook his head definitively. "I didn't go with Lanie."

"And yet she couldn't stop talking about the wonderful lunch you had at a fabulous little café by your hotel."

"We did have lunch together one day," he admitted. "I ran into her in the lobby of the hotel when I was heading out to grab a bite and invited her to join me. It wasn't anything more than that."

"You don't have to explain anything to me," she told him.

"Apparently I do," he said. Because he could tell by the tone of her voice that she'd arrived at her own—and obviously erroneous—conclusions. "Do you really think I was sleeping with another woman the night after I kissed you?"

"I really didn't give it much thought at all," she said, shifting her gaze to the clouds outside the window.

If he hadn't already suspected that she was lying, her refusal to even look at him would have triggered his suspicion. "Yes, I went away with some friends. And yes, I received a couple of offers to hook up while I was there.

"But I didn't consider any of them for more than two seconds—" he shifted so that his shoulder brushed against hers, and lowered his mouth closer to her ear "—because since that kiss we shared under the mistletoe, I haven't been able to go much longer than that without thinking about you.

"And when I think about that kiss, I remember how good

your body felt against mine, and how surprised—and incredibly turned on—I was by the passion of your response."

"You're right," she said shortly. "Our memories are different. But considering that we're going to be working closely together, I think it would be best if we both just forgot about that kiss."

"I already know that I can't," he told her.

"Maybe you just need to try a little harder."

"Are you saying that you have forgotten?"

"I'm saying that I'm not going to let anything interfere with our working relationship."

"I know how to separate business from pleasure," he assured her.

"Let's keep the focus on business," she suggested.

"That doesn't sound like nearly as much fun."

"I like my job and I want to keep my job," she told him. "Which means I'm definitely not going to sleep with my boss."

His lips curved. "I'm not your boss yet."

She lifted a brow. "Your point?"

"We could use the next few weeks to get this…attraction…out of our systems, so that it won't be an impediment to our working together."

"Thank you for that uniquely intriguing offer," she said primly, "but no."

Despite his blatant flirtation on the plane, when they got to the St. Louis store and started to review the books, Nathan proved that he did know how to separate business from pleasure.

Allison was impressed by his knowledge of the company's history and employees and the diligence of his work. She hadn't assumed he was moving into the CFO's office because his name was Garrett, but she had suspected the familial connection had paved the way. Watching him work, she realized that had been her error. Nate was going to be the new CFO because he was the most qualified person for the job.

Still, it took several hours before the discrepancy was found. Working together to match invoices to payment receipts, it became apparent to both Nate and Allison that some numbers had been transposed when the deposit was made. Instead of $53,642 being deposited, the amount was noted as $35,264—a deficit of $18,378. But what seemed like a simple accounting error was further complicated by the facts that the payment had been made in cash (apparently office furniture for an upstart law firm that didn't yet have a checking account) and no one seemed to know where the $18,378 had gone—or they weren't admitting it if they did.

To a company that did hundreds of millions of dollars in business annually, the amount was hardly significant. But the misplacement of any funds, whether careless or deliberate, was unacceptable from an accounting perspective. The head of the store's finance department agreed and promised to locate the missing money before the end of the week.

"I'm surprised you're going to leave it for Bob to deal with," Allison said when they'd left the man's office.

"They're his people," Nate said. "And I have no doubt he already knows who is responsible for making that eighteen thousand dollars disappear."

"So you don't think it was a mistake?"

"I would have believed the transposing of the digits was a mistake if the correct amount had actually been deposited—the fact that it wasn't proves otherwise."

"You don't want to know who did it?"

"I will know," he said confidently. "But I don't need to know today."

"In that case—" she glanced at her watch as they made their way toward the exit "—we should be able to get to the airport in time to catch an earlier flight back to Raleigh."

"That would be good." He stopped to pull his phone out of his pocket and frowned at the message he read. "But I don't think it's going to happen."

"Why not?"

"Apparently a storm has moved into this area. I just got a notification from the airline that our flight has been delayed."

She pulled out her phone and found that she'd received the same message. "There has to be a mistake—the forecast was clear."

"Then the forecast was wrong."

She halted beside him at the glass doors and blinked, as if she didn't quite believe what she was seeing. Or rather *not* seeing, since the blowing snow made it impossible to see anything past it.

Nate was focused on his phone, checking for updates from the airline. "All flights are canceled for the next twelve hours."

"So what are we supposed to do?" She couldn't help but think of the promise she'd made to Dylan that morning.

"Find a hotel," he said easily. "Hopefully one that isn't too far away from where we are right now."

"A hotel?" she echoed.

"Unless you want to bunk down here?"

"Of course not." What she wanted was to be back in Charisma, in her own apartment with her son—not stranded in St. Louis, and especially not with a man who made her feel nothing but heat despite the obviously frigid temperatures outside.

"There's a Courtland not too far from here," he said. "Let me just give them a call and see if we can get a room."

"Two rooms."

But the room situation wasn't really her biggest concern—nor was the fact that she hadn't packed an overnight bag. She was more worried about the fact that she hadn't packed anything for Dylan. Of course, her ex-husband knew that Mrs. Hanson, the widow who lived across the hall from Allison and Dylan, had a spare key and could let him in to get whatever he needed. She just wasn't sure that Jeff would know what their son needed.

Did he know that Dylan had specific pajamas that he liked to wear when he stayed at his dad's house? Would he remember to pack Bear, the little boy's ancient and much-loved teddy bear? Would he make sure that Dylan did his homework? Would he remember to pack his lunch for the next day? She worried about all of those details while Nathan made a phone call to secure their hotel rooms.

Less than five minutes later, they battled the blowing snow and howling wind toward their rental car in the parking lot. Despite the wild weather, Nate went around to the passenger side to open the door for her, an unexpectedly chivalrous gesture that reminded her there was more to the man than his reputation implied.

She slid into her seat and buckled up, aware that the roads were going to be icy and slick—and still not nearly as dangerous as spending the night in a hotel with Nathan Garrett.

Chapter Four

It took nearly twenty-five minutes to travel the six miles between the store and the hotel.

And for every single one of those minutes, Allison was grateful that Nate was behind the wheel. She considered herself a good driver, but she had little experience driving on snow-covered roads and absolutely no experience navigating unfamiliar streets in whiteout conditions.

As Nathan eased to a stop at a red light, he glanced over at her. "Are you okay?"

"Fine. Why?"

"You're clutching your bag so tight your knuckles are white and you haven't said a word since we pulled out of the parking lot."

"I wanted you to be able to focus on the roads."

"I've driven in worse," he assured her.

"Really?"

"I went to New York University," he said.

"You have to be crazy to drive in New York City on a good day."

"A little bit," he agreed, easing into the intersection when the light turned green.

"There's the hotel," Allison said, recognizing the distinctly scripted *C* that was the Courtland trademark.

He pulled into the underground parking garage and found a vacant spot. "At least we won't have to brush snow off in the morning."

"I'm hoping it will all be melted by the morning."

"That's definitely wishful thinking," he told her. "But as long as the storm has passed, we'll get home tomorrow."

She nodded and followed him to the elevator.

"Ever checked into a hotel without a suitcase before?" he asked her.

"No," she said, just a little primly.

He waggled his eyebrows. "Does it make you feel like you're on your way to an illicit rendezvous?"

"No," she said again, because that was something she definitely did *not* want to be thinking about. "I don't do things like that."

"Never?"

"Never."

He flashed that tingle-inducing smile. "Too bad."

When the elevator opened up on the main level of the hotel, he went directly to the check-in desk and spoke to the woman behind the counter. The name on her tag was Sheila, and she smiled warmly at Nate.

Part of the customer service or proof of the effect that he had on all females? And why should she care? He could flirt with the desk clerk and every other female in a ten-block radius, if he wanted—and he probably did. She just wanted to get to her room to make a phone call.

"We're almost at capacity because of a veterinarian medicine conference," she told him. "So we weren't able to find two rooms…"

Allison's breath caught—

"…on the same floor."

—and released.

"We're just happy you were able to accommodate us at all," Nate assured her.

"The storm caught a lot of people unaware," Sheila said. "The phones have been ringing almost nonstop for the past hour as stranded travelers scramble to find beds."

Allison felt a slight twinge of guilt that they were tak-ing two rooms—no doubt each with two beds—until she reminded herself that this wasn't the only hotel in town.

"If I could just get a credit card for each room?" Sheila prompted.

Allison reached for her wallet but Nate was already passing his corporate credit card across the desk. "Put both rooms on this."

"I can pay for my own room," she protested.

"And if this was a vacation, I'd let you," he said. "But this was a business trip, so the hotel is a business expense."

"I don't imagine accounting will be happy to reimburse for two rooms for what was supposed to have been a quick day trip."

His brows lifted. "Are you offering to share a room?"

"No."

He grinned at her immediate and vehement response, then lowered his head and his voice. "I promise—I don't snore."

"I don't care," she assured him.

He lifted one shoulder in a half shrug. "Your loss."

She didn't doubt that it probably was, but she'd learned a long time ago that impulsive actions could have extensive repercussions. She didn't do impulsive anymore.

Sheila came back to the counter. "You're in room 542, Ms. Caldwell, and you're in 913, Mr. Garrett." She passed their respective key cards across the desk. "Neither of you has any luggage?"

"No," Nathan answered for both of them. "Our trip wasn't supposed to be longer than a few hours."

Sheila reached into a drawer and pulled out a couple of clear plastic bags with various sundries, including tooth-brush, toothpaste, comb, cotton swabs, disposable razor and sample size deodorant. "If you need anything else, there's a clothing boutique, general store and pharmacy on the lower level. There's also Prime—our steak and seafood restaurant, the Martini Bar and the Gateway Lounge, so you should be able to find something to suit your palate."

"Thank you," Allison said, gratefully taking the key and kit.

Nathan followed her to the elevator. "Are you hungry?"

"Starved," she admitted.

He pressed the buttons for five and nine. "Do you want to try the restaurant?"

Her stomach growled at the thought of a thick, juicy steak, but her mind warned of the dangers of enjoying a cozy dinner with her sexy boss. "I'll probably just grab a sandwich from the lounge and eat in my room."

His brow furrowed. "A sandwich? Really?"

She felt her cheeks flush. "I've got some phone calls to make."

"I do, too." He glanced at his watch. "Let's meet back downstairs at six."

She'd never said she would have dinner with him; he'd just steamrolled over her protests. Of course, he was accustomed to being the man in charge at the office—and probably in his relationships. And although she instinctively balked at the take-charge attitude that was far too reminiscent of her ex-husband's demeanor, she realized that he was paying for her room and most likely her dinner, too, which made it a business dinner. It wasn't as if he was asking—or demanding—that she go on a date with him.

"Six-thirty," she finally relented when the bell chimed to announce their arrival on the fifth floor. "I'll meet you downstairs then."

The first call she made was to her ex-husband, to tell Jeff that she was stuck in St. Louis. Since it was past the time that he should have picked up Dylan from school, she frowned when the call went immediately to voice mail. She left a message, asking him to call her back when he had a chance. After that, she spent some time responding to emails that had come in throughout the day, periodically glancing at her silent phone as if she could will it to ring.

Dylan had mentioned that Jillian had dance and Jocelyn had piano—or was it vice versa? She never seemed to be able to keep the girls' activities straight, which wasn't relevant anyway. What was relevant was that she'd never known Jeff not to have his phone literally attached to his hip. And with each minute that passed, her anxiousness increased. In the absence of any response from her ex-husband, how could she even be certain that he'd picked their son up from school?

Logically, she knew that the school would have called if Dylan had been left there. But the boy had been in an obviously disgruntled mood that morning—disgruntled enough to leave the school yard on his own? She didn't think so, but it was hard to remain rational when she was so far away and helpless to do anything but wait for Jeff to respond to her message.

Well, not entirely helpless. She picked up her phone again and called her apartment, neither surprised nor reassured when the answering machine clicked on. She considered trying Mrs. Hanson to ask if she'd seen Dylan, but she didn't want to worry her elderly neighbor unnecessarily. Because although Allison was worried, she acknowledged that she might be overreacting to the situation.

Instead of calling Mrs. Hanson, she tried Jeff's number again—and got his voice mail again. Then she called a number she very rarely dialed: her ex-husband's new home.

Jodie answered, sounding breathless and annoyed, on the fifth ring. "'Lo?"

"Hi, Jodie. It's Allison."

The other woman huffed out a breath. "This really isn't a good time—I'm trying to get little Jefferson down for a nap and he'd just started to drift off when the phone rang."

In the background, she could hear distant crying. "I'm sorry," she apologized automatically, "but I haven't been able to reach Jeff and I wanted to make sure he remembered to pick up Dylan from school."

"Of course he remembered."

"Usually he sends me a text to confirm."

"Well, usually we don't have three kids needing to be in three different places and then, on top of all of that, you dumped Dylan on him without even asking if it was convenient, so perhaps he was just a little busy."

Allison bit her tongue so hard she thought she might draw blood. When she could finally speak without letting loose on her ex-husband's new wife, she only said, "In case he doesn't get the voice mail message I left for him—" she didn't admit that she'd left three "—can you ask him to give me a call when he gets in?"

"Sure. But aren't you supposed to be here to pick Dylan up in a couple of hours?"

"That was the original plan," she agreed. "But a snowstorm stranded me in St. Louis."

"Oh." Somehow there was a wealth of disapproval—and accusation—in that single syllable. "I guess that means he'll be staying here tonight."

"Since Family Services generally frowns upon eight-year-olds being left alone when a parent is out of town, I guess it does," she confirmed.

"I'll make sure Jefferson gives you a call."

"Thank you." Allison disconnected and blew out a breath.

She was generally an easygoing person who liked almost everyone, but no matter how hard she'd tried—and she really had tried—she'd never managed to like Jodie Daley-Caldwell.

From day one, her ex-husband's new wife had treated Allison as though she was "the other woman." Yes, Jeff and Jodie had dated all through high school, but they'd gone to different colleges after graduation and decided to end their relationship shortly after that. It was more than two years later before Allison even met Jeff, so she could hardly be accused of coming between them.

And while she might have had nothing to do with their breakup, her marriage to Jeff had certainly been an impediment to their reconciliation, albeit one that he'd quickly rectified when he realized he was still in love with his high school sweetheart. Allison knew that Jodie wished she could pretend her husband's first marriage had never happened—but Dylan's existence and regular visitation with his father made that impossible. And Allison couldn't help but resent her son's stepmother treating him like he was an inconvenience.

She was still trying to shake off the weight of the conversation when a knock sounded at the door. Frowning, she squinted through the peephole to find Nathan standing outside her room.

Drawing in another deep breath, she opened the door. "I thought we were meeting downstairs."

"I wanted to make sure you didn't change your mind."

"Was changing my mind an option?"

"No," he admitted. "Which is why I'm at your door."

She still hadn't talked to either Jeff or Dylan, but they both had her cell phone number so she didn't have to wait in the room for a return call. And although she knew she wouldn't completely relax until she'd heard from her son, she tucked her key card in the pocket of her blazer, slung her purse over her shoulder and stepped out into the hall.

Reassured that Dylan was safely in his father's care, the knots of anxiety in her belly hadn't dissipated but they did loosen enough to make her realize how very hungry she was.

Then Nate put his hand on her back to guide her toward the elevator, and the awareness that her stomach was empty was supplanted by an entirely different awareness.

Over the six years that Allison had been John Garrett's executive assistant, she'd gotten to know her boss very well and she'd never felt the least bit uncomfortable with him. Of course, she'd never been kissed by him the way Nathan had kissed her at the Christmas party.

Which had been more than four weeks ago. Not exactly ancient history in her world, but certainly enough time had passed that the memory of it shouldn't still make her pulse race. Except that it did. And standing beside Nate in the elevator, just the two of them in the confined space, her pulse was definitely racing.

When they arrived on the main floor, he gestured for her to precede him, then he splayed his hand on her back again. She was wearing a silk shell and a tailored jacket, but she was as aware of his touch as if there was no fabric barrier between his wide palm and her bare skin.

The restaurant hostess led them to their table, and she noticed that the larger booths had rectangular tables and straight bench-style seating on three sides; the smaller booths had round tables with semi-circular bench seating designed to allow couples to snuggle close together if they chose.

Allison sat as far away from Nate as possible. But even then, the curved design of the booth and the flickering candle on the table provided a romantic ambience that she didn't want to feel. The hostess handed them menus, recited the daily specials and promised that Stefano would be right over to take their drink orders.

She opened her menu and skimmed the offerings, wondering why it felt so much like a date when it clearly wasn't. She was here with Nate only because they were stranded. As soon as the storm blew over—please God, let it be gone by the morning—they would be on their way back to North Carolina and their separate lives. But while they were stuck in St. Louis, they were having dinner together only because they both had to eat. It absolutely was *not* a date.

"Red or white?"

The question seemed to come from out of nowhere, and she looked up at Nate. "Sorry?"

"Wine," he clarified.

"Oh. Um." She figured adding wine to the situation could only equal trouble, so she looked at the waiter with an apologetic smile. "I'll just have a glass of water."

"And a bottle of the Woodbridge cabernet sauvignon," Nate said.

"Good choice, sir," Stefano said, then retreated to get their beverages.

"Do you know what you want?" Nate asked.

She forced her gaze to stay focused on the menu. "The peppercorn sirloin sounds good."

"It does," he agreed. "I was looking at the same thing."

The waiter returned with two glasses of ice water and the bottle of wine. Stefano deftly popped the cork and poured a sample for Nate to approve. He sipped, savored, nodded.

Stefano, apparently having forgotten as quickly as Nate that she'd said she didn't want any wine, tipped the bottle over her glass. She decided it was ridiculous to worry that a single glass of wine was going to override all of her inhibitions and entice her to drag her soon-to-be boss into her hotel room to have her way with him.

But she picked up the glass of water first.

"Are you ready to order?"

Allison went with the peppercorn sirloin—medium well, with a side of wild rice and a green salad. Nate opted for the ten-ounce sirloin—medium, with a baked potato, fully loaded and cauliflower au gratin.

When the waiter had gone, Nate offered her the bread basket, but she shook her head.

"I know we worked through lunch," he said, as he tore open a warm multigrain roll. "So how are you not starving?"

"I am," she admitted. "But I'm waiting for my steak."

"I'm just glad to see that you aren't one of those women who thinks that lettuce is a meal."

"Why would my eating habits be of any concern to you?"

He broke off a piece of bread and popped it in his mouth. "Because now I know that, when I finally convince you to go out with me, I can take you to a real restaurant and not just a salad bar."

"You definitely don't need to worry about that, because I wouldn't go out with you."

He didn't argue, he just smiled.

That smug, sexy smile that made her realize he could probably convince her of anything if he made the slightest effort.

She tried to remember all of the reasons that getting involved with him on a personal level was a very bad idea—most notably that the man was going to be her boss and an affair would do nothing to enhance her credibility in the office. Focusing her attention on the forthcoming changes at Garrett Furniture, she said, "How do you think your uncle is going to adjust to retirement?"

"Reluctantly," Nate admitted. "My aunt Ellen has been pressuring him to retire for the better part of four years, and he kept saying he would, and then he kept putting it off."

"He can't put it off any longer."

"It certainly doesn't look that way. But there are still two more weeks before the end of the month, so I'm not rearranging the furniture in his office just yet."

Beneath the words, she heard just a hint of the frustration that had been building over those four years since he'd been brought back to Charisma in preparation of taking over the position. "For what it's worth, he has no doubts about your abilities to do the job."

"Then why did he keep postponing his retirement?"

"Because he's sure that he'll go crazy inside of two

weeks." She smiled in response to the lift of his brows. "His words."

"Aunt Ellen will probably drive him crazy," Nate acknowledged. "She'll make him eat a heart-healthy diet to stay alive, but she'll drive him crazy."

Despite the disparaging words, she heard the affection in his voice.

Over the years that she'd worked for John Garrett, she'd learned that the company history was also family history. Garrett Furniture was founded almost sixty years earlier by Henry Garrett, who worked in the tobacco fields during the day and puttered with wood in his workshop at night. His first project was a dining room table and chairs for his family; then he designed and built a cabinet for his wife to display the heirloom china that had come down to her from her grandmother.

Visitors, friends and family alike, were usually surprised to learn that he'd made the furniture that filled the home, and he was soon being asked to make pieces for others. A few years later, he quit his job in the tobacco fields to focus on building furniture full time. A few more years after that, the first Garrett Furniture store opened.

When he finally retired—forced to do so because of hands that were so twisted with arthritis, he could no longer hold the tools that had built his business—he turned the reins over to three of his sons: David, John and Thomas. (A fourth son, Edward, had gone to medical school up north and, after graduation, settled down to practice in Pinehurst, New York.)

David was the CEO, John was the CFO and Thomas was the COO. Allison thought it was interesting that each of the men had three children, and while some of those offspring had chosen to do other things—David's son, Daniel, had been a network security specialist before he decided to invest in a stock car racing team; John's son, Justin, was an ER doctor; and Thomas's daughter, Jordyn, was the manager of O'Reilly's Pub—most worked for Garrett Furniture in one capacity or another. And despite their large number and disparate career choices, they were a close family. They all came together for the company Christmas party, the annual summer picnic and countless birthdays and anniversaries and weddings. (The three cousins in Pinehurst—Matthew, a surgeon; Jackson, an attorney; and Lukas, a veterinarian— had all married within the past couple of years.)

Stefano delivered their plates, and they each dug into their meals with enthusiasm. Between bites, Allison sipped the wine in her glass. She was halfway through her steak when Nate asked, "What are you worrying about now?"

"Why do you think I'm worried?"

"Because you've got that little line—" he touched a finger to illustrate the spot between his own brows "—you get when you're worried about something."

She was surprised by both his observation and insight, and she couldn't deny that she was worried. "I wasn't able to get in touch with Jeff to let him know that I wasn't going to be back tonight."

"Who's Jeff?" he asked.

"My ex-husband."

Above those warm, smoky eyes, his brows lifted. "Why would your ex-husband care that you're stuck out of town?"

"It probably won't bother him as much as it will bother Jodie," she admitted. "Because they weren't planning on keeping Dylan overnight."

He speared a floret with his fork. "And Dylan is?"

"My son."

Chapter Five

Nate paused with the fork halfway to his mouth and tried to absorb what she'd just told him.

My son.

The words echoed through his mind like a clanging bell—an unmistakable warning.

He'd always appreciated all kinds of women. It didn't matter to him if they were blonde, brunette or redhead, skinny or curvy, tall or short. He didn't have any specific type—except that women who were tied down by familial obligations were definitely *not* his type.

And Allison Caldwell had a kid.

He popped the cauliflower into his mouth and tried to wrap his mind around the fact that the sexy woman seated across from him had carried and borne a child.

How had he not known that she was a mother? It seemed unlikely to him that the existence of her son hadn't come up in conversation at some time over the past four years. Or maybe it had, and he just hadn't paid much attention.

When he'd first moved back to Charisma, he couldn't help but notice that his uncle had a new executive assistant—or that she was young and very attractive. He also knew that his transfer to the head office of Garrett Furniture was a huge step up the corporate ladder and, determined to focus on his career, he'd made every effort to steer clear of the temptation that was Allison Caldwell.

The fact that she had a kid was just one more—and possibly the biggest—reason that he should walk away from her. A better man would claim that revelation didn't change anything. Nate had never claimed to be a better man. And even though both of his brothers had wives and children, he wasn't eager to go down that same path.

He had no interest, not right now or in the foreseeable future, in doing the whole family thing. If he had a choice—and he did—he would avoid getting tangled up with a woman who was already tangled up by domestic responsibilities.

He cut off a piece of steak, chewed. He knew that being a mother was more than a title; it was an intrinsic part of a woman's identity. But when Allison had been in his arms, responding to his kiss with a passion that matched his own, he knew without a doubt she sure as heck hadn't been thinking or feeling like a mother.

The fact that she had a child did nothing to dampen his desire for her, but it did make him realize that pursuing a relationship with her would be more complicated than he'd imagined. Maybe more complicated than he wanted.

With the exceptions of only his niece and his nephew, kids were way outside of his comfort zone. Although he hadn't completely disregarded the possibility that he might want one or more of his own someday, that someday was somewhere in the distant future. And even then, he wasn't sure he wanted to take on the responsibility of someone else's kid—no matter how much he wanted the kid's mother.

"How old is he?" he asked.

"Eight. Almost nine."

Which was older than he'd expected, but still young enough that the kid would be the focus of most of her time and attention. "You must have been young when you had him."

"Not yet twenty-two," she confirmed.

"Were you married then?"

She nodded. "We got married in September. Dylan was born in March. Our divorce was final two years after that."

"It must have been hard for your son, being so young when you split."

"Actually, I've always thought it was good that because Dylan was so young, our separation wasn't a big traumatic event in his life. In fact, he has no memories of his dad and me together." She picked up her glass of wine and sipped. "Of course, our marriage was so brief—and so chaotic as we struggled to get used to being married and dealing with a brand-new baby—that *I* barely have any memories of his dad and me together."

"Do you still love him?" He wasn't sure why he asked the question, why her response mattered to him, but it did.

"I never really did," she admitted. "We were just a couple of college kids who weren't always vigilant about birth control yet somehow naive enough to be shocked when I ended up pregnant.

"Jeff asked me to marry him because he felt it was the right thing to do, and I accepted his proposal because marrying a guy I didn't know all that well was a slightly less terrifying prospect than having and raising a child on my own.

"He's a good dad," she said. "At least, he tries to be. He picks Dylan up from school every Wednesday and has him overnight every other weekend, but he doesn't often make extracurricular activities or school events because he's got another family now."

"He's remarried?"

"Exchanged vows with his high school sweetheart only a few days after our divorce was final."

Her tone was neutral, almost too neutral, making him suspect that she'd been more hurt by the event than her matter-of-fact statement revealed.

"That was—" so many words came to mind: cold, cruel and heartless were only a few, but he settled on "—quick."

She smiled at that. "Yes," she agreed. "But not really surprising. Because even when he asked me to marry him, he was still in love with her. Of course, I didn't know that until after we split up." She frowned into her glass of wine, as if it was somehow responsible for her rambling. "I'm sorry—I don't know why I'm telling you this."

"I asked," he reminded her.

"And now I'll bet you're sorry you did."

"Not at all. I'm just surprised that I've known you for more than four years and never knew that you had a child."

"I guess you're not the only one who knows how to separate business and pleasure." She glanced away as her cell phone vibrated on the table. Whatever she saw on the screen made her lips curve in a smile that was as quick as it was genuine.

"Your son?" he guessed.

She nodded. "Excuse me," she said, and rose from the table to answer the call.

Allison was as relieved as she was pleased to hear Dylan's voice. Not just to know for sure that he was okay, but because the call gave her an excuse to step away from the table and the seductive gaze of Nathan Garrett.

"Hi, honey. How was school today?"

Dylan ignored her question to ask his own. "Where are you?"

"I'm still in St. Louis."

"You said you were going to pick me up," he reminded her, his tone querulous.

"I didn't know that they were going to close the airport because of a snowstorm."

"It's not snowing here."

"Remember when we looked at the map this morning?" she asked him. "Missouri is a long way from North Carolina."

"I don't wanna stay here tonight. Why can't I have a sleepover at Aunt Chelsea's?"

It wasn't so long ago that he used to love going to his dad's, staying at his dad's, but that was before he had to share his dad's attention with three other kids. "Because she has a class on Thursdays and, even if she didn't, it's too late to make other arrangements."

On the other end of the line, her son was silent.

"Did your dad take you home to get your overnight bag?"

"Yeah. And he made me pack extra stuff 'cause he said I'm gonna stay for the whole weekend, but I was here last weekend."

"I know," she acknowledged. "But your dad and Jodie are going to be out of town next week so they asked if they could change the dates."

"You could've said no," he told her.

Yes, she could have, but she tried to be accommodating, to ensure that her son got as much time as possible with his father. But there were times she couldn't help but feel that her ex-husband took advantage of her flexibility without regard to their son's schedule or his feelings.

"We'll do something special next weekend when we're together," she promised.

"Like what?"

"I don't know what. Why don't you think on it and we'll discuss some ideas when you get home?"

"You mean when you get home."

"Sure," she agreed. Provided it stopped snowing overnight, she should be home the next day, and then she would have two nights alone before he got back on Sunday. But she didn't want to think about that when she was already missing him so much.

"Where are you now?" he asked. "Are you on the airplane?"

"No, I'm at a hotel near the airport."

"You don't have Bear," he said. "'Cause he was still in my bed when Dad took me home to get my stuff."

As a baby, Dylan wouldn't go to sleep unless his favorite teddy bear was in his crib. As he got older, he grew less dependent but still usually packed the toy when he would be gone overnight. And a couple of years earlier, he'd started packing Bear in his mom's suitcase whenever she had to go away, so she wouldn't be lonely.

"I didn't bring Bear because I didn't think I would have to stay overnight," she reminded him.

"I wish you had him with you, so you don't have to sleep alone."

It was the innocent suggestion of a child, but his words brought to mind all kinds of not-so-innocent possibilities.

Maybe she should consider Nathan's offer to get the attraction out of their systems—except she was no longer certain the offer was on the table. She could tell that he'd been taken aback to learn she had a child, and she suspected the revelation had diminished the attraction—at least on his part.

"I'll be okay by myself," she promised him.

"I love you, Mom."

"I love you, too, Dilly Bug."

As she disconnected the call and tucked her phone into the pocket of her jacket, she heard the echo of Chelsea's voice in the back of her mind.

How long has it been since you've had sex?

She honestly wasn't sure. She'd had only two lovers in the six years that had passed since she'd divorced, and neither had been anything more than a temporary diversion. She hadn't wanted anything more. And she didn't want anything more now, but she couldn't deny that being with Nathan Garrett made her want.

Bad idea, she reminded herself sternly as she made her way back to the table.

When she got there, Stefano was clearing away their plates.

He asked if they wanted dessert and coffee; she declined the former but accepted the latter. Nate ordered the New York–style cheesecake with chocolate-cookie crust and strawberry-Grand Marnier topping.

When it came, the square plate was drizzled with chocolate sauce and sprinkled with powdered sugar, with the thick slice of cake at its center. There were also two forks.

"Try it," Nate instructed.

She couldn't deny that she was tempted—and annoyed with Nate for putting the temptation so squarely in front of her. "Do you ever take no for an answer?"

He smiled at the frustration in her tone. "It's just cheesecake."

And he was right, but she was afraid if she didn't say no and mean it now, she wouldn't be able to say no to anything else that he asked of her.

He picked up one of the forks, broke off a piece of the cake and held it toward her.

"I said I didn't want any dessert."

"Your lips are saying no but your eyes are saying yes."

She rolled her eyes at the cliché, but she couldn't deny that it was true. She loved cheesecake, and her mouth was practically watering in anticipation of the rich, creamy flavor, but she kept her lips firmly closed.

"Are you always this stubborn?" he asked.

"How is refusing dessert stubborn?"

He moved the fork away from her lips and slid it between his own. "You're denying yourself something that you want for no reason other than to be difficult."

"You ordered the cake—I would think you'd be happy not to share it."

"Food is a necessity, but dessert is a pleasure. And pleasure—" he scooped up another bite "—should be shared."

"Are we still talking about cheesecake?"

His eyes held hers as he guided the fork closer to her mouth. "You tell me."

He was temptation personified, and she could no longer resist.

Her lips parted, and he slid the fork between them. Her eyes closed and a hum of satisfaction echoed in her throat.

"It's good, isn't it?"

She held up a hand. "I'm having a moment."

He chuckled softly and nudged the plate closer to her.

She picked up the second fork and took another bite of the cake, savoring the creaminess of the cake and the sweetness of the strawberries on her tongue.

"This is—" she couldn't find words that would adequately describe the taste "—even better than sex."

Which was not something she ever intended to say out loud—especially not in front of Nate Garrett.

His only response was a lift of his eyebrows as he took another bite of the dessert. "It's very good," he confirmed. "But if you think it's better than sex, you need a different partner."

"Or at least a partner."

He picked up his coffee. "That would be a good start."

She shook her head. "And that is why I usually don't have more than one glass of wine—because I lose the filter between my brain and my mouth."

"I like you like this," he said. "Saying what you're thinking instead of censoring your thoughts and weighing your words."

"Lillian—my former mother-in-law—used to admonish me all the time for speaking without thinking."

"Because your thoughts weren't in line with hers?"

"Because *Mrs.* Jefferson Caldwell the Third didn't have any thoughts that didn't echo those of *Mr.* Jefferson Caldwell the Third. And, if I was ever going to be a good Southern wife, I needed to take my cues from my husband."

"Jefferson Caldwell the Fourth?" he guessed.

She nodded.

"I'll bet you didn't score any points by choosing a name for your son that wasn't Jefferson Caldwell the Fifth."

"You'd be right," she agreed. "But what else could they expect from a Yankee?"

"You're not a North Carolina native?"

"I was born there, but my parents weren't. They moved from New Jersey shortly after they were married."

"Do your parents still live in the area?"

She shook her head. "I was an only child born long after they'd given up hope of ever having a baby. My dad was a heavy smoker for almost forty years and died of lung cancer when I was in high school, and my mom suffered a fatal heart attack a few years after that, before Dylan was born. Which means that my former in-laws are the only grandparents he has. Unfortunately, they weren't ever able to forgive me for getting pregnant—or Dylan for being the product of that unplanned pregnancy."

He frowned at that. "You're kidding."

She shook her head. "Jeff dated Jodie all through high school. They lived in the same neighborhood growing up. Their mothers were best friends. Everyone expected they would be together forever. Jeff went to UNC Wilmington for occupational therapy; Jodie went to Asheville to study music. Halfway through their first year, they broke up.

"I met Jeff when I was in my third year of economics at the Cameron School of Business, and a few months later, I got pregnant. But now, much to Lillian's delight, Jefferson and Jodie are together again—happily married and the doting parents of Jocelyn, Jillian and Jefferson the Fifth."

"For real?"

"As if I'd make something like that up."

"How does your son feel about his dad's other family?"

"It is what it is," she said. "When Jeff first got remarried, he was great about spending as much time as he could with Dylan. When Jeff and Jodie bought their house, Dylan got to help decorate his room and he loved going there for sleepovers. Then Jodie had a baby and all of their attention shifted. But Dylan doted on his little sister and—fifteen months later—his second little sister, too.

"Then Jefferson the Fifth was born. Instead of making the girls share a room, they put the crib in Dylan's room, since—as Jeff explained—he's not there all the time anyway. Which wouldn't have been a big deal except that his race car posters were taken down and a mural of a big orange giraffe with a balloon bouquet was painted on the wall."

"Race car posters?"

"Dylan's a huge racing fan," she told him. "Even when he was in kindergarten, the age when most kids wake up early Saturday morning to watch cartoons, he was watching race highlights on the sports channel."

He smiled at that. "Has he ever been to a race?"

"His dad's taken him to a couple of amateur races at the dirt track outside of Charisma."

"Stock car racing isn't your thing?"

"I don't mind watching it on occasion, but I don't understand all the lingo, and Dylan usually ends up rolling his eyes when he tries to talk to me about bump drafting or restrictive plates."

"Restrictor plates," Nate corrected.

She shook her head. "I still have no idea what they are."

"Metal plates with holes in them, installed at the intake of an engine to limit its power."

"But why would you want to limit its power?"

"To slow it down."

"Which doesn't make any sense to me," she confided.

"Isn't the whole point of a race to go fast? Isn't that how you win?"

"Sure," he agreed. "But on super speedways, the use of restrictor plates is designed to reduce the number of high-speed crashes."

"I guess I'll have to take your word for it."

"So if stock car racing isn't your thing—what is?"

"I don't know that I really have a thing," she hedged.

"Everyone has something," he insisted. "Like skydiving or stamp collecting, foreign films or French cuisine."

Her brows lifted. "Are those your hobbies?"

He laughed. "I like football and baseball. I prefer movies with action and explosions and thick steaks cooked on the grill. I also like camping under the stars, classic rock played loud and big, slobbery dogs."

"That's an impressive list."

"Now it's your turn," he told her.

She considered for a minute. "I can't stand football but I don't mind baseball, I like walking barefoot in the sand, the scent of freshly cut grass, movies that make me laugh, books that make me cry, dinner by candlelight, dark chocolate, red wine, spring flowers, small dogs, big hugs and the sound of a baby's laugh."

He nodded approvingly. "That recital of facts told me something else about you."

"What's that?"

"You're competitive."

"How do you figure?"

"You had to make sure your list was longer than mine."

"It's not the size of the list that matters—it's the self-awareness." Though her tone was solemn, the sparkle in her eye told him that she was teasing.

And while he wasn't sure about the "self" part, he was definitely aware of her.

He understood why she didn't want to get involved with

him. He'd thought her reservations centered on an unwillingness to complicate their working relationship, but he knew now that her reasons went deeper than that. And while he couldn't deny the validity of those reasons, he still wasn't ready to back off.

Yeah, the kid was a complication. But the kid was in North Carolina, while he and Allison were stranded together in St. Louis. And it had been a long time since he'd been so completely and thoroughly captivated by a woman.

He'd often found himself attracted to a pretty face and womanly curves, and although Allison had both, she also had a sharp mind, a sense of humor and an honest sincerity that was, in his experience, far too rare.

"So if a man wanted to impress you, he should bring you a bouquet of tulips and take you out for a candlelight dinner?"

"That would be a good start," she agreed. "Except that I don't date."

He signed the check that Stefano delivered. "Ever?"

"Rarely. And I'm definitely not going to date my boss."

"I'm not your boss yet," he pointed out to her.

"But you're the VP of Finance of the company that signs my paychecks."

"Chelsea warned me that would be an issue for you." He pushed his chair away from the table and stood.

"Chelsea needs to mind her own business."

"She likes me," he said mildly, offering his hand to her. "In fact, most people do."

After a moment's hesitation, she put her hand in his and rose to her feet. "Yeah, I've heard that."

"Have you ever considered the possibility that my reputation might be the tiniest bit exaggerated?"

"No," she admitted. "Because your reputation isn't really any of my concern."

He guided her into the elevator. "It is if it's a factor in your refusal to go out with me."

"Only one of many."

He rubbed his thumb over the back of her hand, tracing the ridges and valleys of her knuckles in a slow, sensual caress. "Such as the fact that you're not attracted to me?"

She tugged her hand away. "Attraction is nothing more than a trick played by our hormones."

"You can't really believe that."

"Actually, I do," she told him. "And if a relationship is built on nothing but physical attraction, there's nothing left when that attraction fizzles."

"You're letting your experience with your ex-husband color your judgment."

"Perhaps," she acknowledged.

"There's something between us, Allison. Maybe it's attraction, maybe it's more, but I think we need to figure it out."

She watched the lights above the doors indicate their ascension toward the fifth floor. "The only thing we need to do is to work together."

"And we will." He stepped closer to her. "But right now, I want to kiss you."

Her fingers tightened around the key card in her hand, so much that the edges of the plastic dug into her palm. She wanted to shove him away, to distance herself from the temptation that was Nate. But even more than she wanted him gone, she wanted him to kiss her. She knew that she shouldn't, that even one kiss could be dangerous. But she was lonely and he was so damn sexy and just being in close proximity to him made her blood hum.

"There's no mistletoe this time," he told her. "No reason or explanation aside from the fact that I haven't been able to think about anything else since I kissed you at the party."

His tone was as seductive as the words, weaving a spell around her, drawing her in.

"But if you don't want me to, just say the words and I'll walk away."

She wanted to say them—she *needed* to say them. But when she opened her mouth, the words refused to come. Because the truth was, she *did* want him to kiss her. She wanted to feel the way she'd felt the night of the Christmas party, when he'd taken her in his arms and held her as if he'd never let her go. When he'd kissed her as if he could go on kissing her forever.

She laid her palms on his chest, where she could feel the beating of his heart—strong and steady—and moistened her lips with her tongue. "I don't want you to walk away," she admitted. "I want you to kiss me, but I'm afraid it won't end there."

"I'm not going to push for more than you're ready to give."

The steady gaze and sincere tone convinced her that he meant what he'd said, but his promise did nothing to reassure her. Because she knew that it wouldn't take much persuasion for her to give him anything, everything.

And then he tipped her chin up and lowered his head. His lips brushed against hers softly, gently. It was a tantalizing caress more than a kiss, an invitation rather than a demand. She responded. Her hands slid over his shoulders to link behind his neck as his lips continued to move over hers, tempting, teasing.

The need started low in her belly, then spread through her veins. His hands moved over her, hotly, hungrily, and everywhere he touched, she burned. She could feel the press of his arousal against her, and thrilled in the knowledge that he wanted her as much as she wanted him. And she did want him—she couldn't deny that simple truth any longer.

He lifted his mouth from hers when the elevator dinged to announce its arrival on the fifth floor. "I'm sorry," he said.

She touched a hand to lips that were still trembling.

"Not for kissing you," he quickly clarified. "For pushing when I said I wouldn't."

"You didn't push," she assured him. "But I did promise myself that I wouldn't invite you into my room."

"Then I should let you get to bed," he said, holding the elevator doors open.

"Wait." She laid a hand on his arm, felt the tension practically vibrating in his muscle. She hadn't realized how much effort it took for him to hold his desire in check, and how much she wanted to unleash it.

She drew in a deep breath and looked up at him. The heat in his gaze burned straight to her core, but she held it without flinching and stepped forward, breaching the distance he'd deliberately put between them.

"Allison," he said, and her name on his lips was as much a warning as a plea.

Her hand slid down his forearm, her fingers skimming over the sleeve of his jacket to link with his.

"I promised that I wouldn't invite you into my room," she said again. "But I didn't promise that I wouldn't go back to yours."

Chapter Six

The elevator seemed to take forever to reach the ninth floor.

Realistically, Nate knew it couldn't have been more than a minute or two, but it felt like forever. He held his breath as the seconds ticked away, certain that each second that passed would be the second that Allison announced she'd changed her mind. He really didn't want her to change her mind.

She squeezed his hand, whether seeking or offering reassurance, he didn't know. But when he glanced into the warmth of those chocolate-colored eyes, he couldn't deny that he wanted her as he hadn't wanted any woman in a very long time.

"You're not having second thoughts, are you?"

"No," she assured him. "But I do think we should establish some ground rules."

She was wearing a silky purple top beneath a belted black blazer and slim-fitting black pants. The material was dark but sheer enough that he could see the lace edging of a camisole. He couldn't wait to strip away her clothes to admire what she wore beneath. He was hoping for a thong to go with the lacy camisole. For all he knew, she might wear white cotton granny panties, but it was his fantasy, so he was going with the thong.

"Nate?" she prompted, as they exited onto his floor.

"Ground rules," he echoed.

She nodded. "If we're going to do this, we should be clear on a few things first."

"What kind of things?"

"That this can be nothing more than a moment stolen from our normal lives. Not only will it not happen again, we won't even mention it when we go back to Charisma."

He slid his key card into the slot; the light blinked green. "You want a one-night stand?"

"It's the only way this will work."

"Why do you say that?" he asked, more curious than offended.

"Because my life in Charisma is complicated enough without adding a relationship—however casual or temporary—to the mix. And aside from that, at the end of the month, you're going to be promoted and there is no way I'm going to be the clichéd secretary screwing around with her boss."

"You can be the sexy executive assistant screwing around with her boss," Nate said, unfastening her jacket and slipping it off of her shoulders.

"No." She tugged at the knot of his tie. "Not going to happen."

His hands found their way under the silky top, his palms gliding up her sides. "So you want to ensure that I don't have any expectations?"

"I just want to be sure that we're in agreement." Her fingers worked the buttons of his shirt.

"I do have one question."

"What's that?"

"If we're only going to have one night, can you stop talking so that we can get to it?"

She laughed softly. "Okay, Mr. Garrett, show me what you've got."

Then she reached between them and stroked the hard length of him. The touch of her hand, even through the fabric, made him suck in a breath.

He lowered his head to capture her mouth. "Nate," he

admonished, nibbling on her bottom lip. "I want to hear you say it."

"Nate." She stroked him again. "I want you, Nate."

"Well, that's convenient—because I want you, too." He unhooked her pants and pushed them over her hips to pool at her feet. Allison stepped out of them and kicked them away.

She wasn't wearing a thong, after all, but a skimpy lace bikini. He wasn't disappointed—and that was even before he saw the thigh-high stockings. He whisked the purple top over her head, dropped it on top of the pile of discarded clothing on the floor, then took a step back. She was still wearing the camisole and panties, stockings and heels, and just looking at her made his mouth water.

"You are…so…beautiful."

She shook her head. "I have stretch marks and small—"

He touched a finger to her lips, silencing her words. "Beautiful," he said again. "Perfect."

Her cheeks colored, as if she was unaccustomed to hearing such words. He wondered what was wrong with the men she'd dated that they obviously hadn't appreciated who she was—and what was wrong with him, that he'd overlooked her for so long.

He was determined to make up for that oversight now.

He lowered his head and touched his lips to the racing pulse point beneath her ear. Then his lips skimmed down her throat, across her collarbone, over the gentle curve of her breast. The tips of her nipples pushed against the lacy fabric, as if begging for his attention. He was more than happy to give it. He traced circles around one rigid peak with his thumb, the other with his tongue, and felt her shudder.

He had a feeling it wasn't going to take much to push either of them to the brink, but he didn't want it to be over fast. He wanted their lovemaking to last all night, and he wanted to savor every minute. If they could have only this one night, he was determined to make sure it was a night she'd never forget.

So while he wanted nothing more than to lay her back down on the bed and bury himself in the wet heat between her thighs—

He sat up abruptly and swore.

Allison propped herself onto her elbows. "What's wrong?"

"I'm not in the habit of carrying condoms in my wallet anymore," he admitted. "And I didn't anticipate that this would happen."

She let out a long, unsteady breath. "I didn't plan for this to happen, either."

"There's a pharmacy downstairs," he remembered. "Just give me five minutes—"

"Wait." She slid out of bed, taking the sheet with her, and rummaged in her purse. "I didn't plan for this," she said again, "but I decided a long time ago that one unplanned pregnancy was enough."

He took the condom she handed to him. "Just one?"

"I have a couple more, but I didn't think you'd need more than one at a time."

"No," he confirmed. "I just wanted to know if I'd have to make a trip to the pharmacy."

Her brows lifted. "Maybe tales of your stamina haven't been exaggerated."

He pulled her into his arms and tossed the sheet aside. "You can let me know later."

She had a moment to wonder: What was she doing? Why was she letting herself believe that sleeping with her soon-to-be boss could be anything but an unmitigated disaster?

Then he kissed her, and all the doubts and recriminations faded away. She couldn't think about anything but how much she wanted this—how much she wanted *him*.

Especially when he eased his lips from hers to ask, "Okay?"

The fact that he did ask, that he was giving her the opportunity to make a different choice even at this late stage of the game, reassured her that this was the right choice. The only choice. Even if they couldn't have more than this one night.

"Okay," she confirmed.

His lips curved, and her insides twisted into knots that were equal parts anticipation and apprehension. It had been a really long time since she'd been naked with a man, and her almost-thirty-year-old body wasn't as sleek and firm as it had been ten years ago. Then he kissed her, and she stopped wondering why he would want her and let herself enjoy the fact that he did.

He lifted his mouth from hers to strip her camisole over her head, push her panties over her hips and roll her stockings down her legs. Then he got rid of his own clothes, kicking off his shoes and socks, tossing his shirt and pants on the floor with hers. But he kept his briefs on, though they barely contained the impressive bulge of his erection.

She reached a hand out, wanting to touch, but he caught her wrist, circling it with his fingers.

"You convinced me that pleasure should be shared," she reminded him.

"And it will be," he promised, easing her back onto the bed. "Soon."

But first he kissed her again, long and slow and deep. And while his mouth patiently and thoroughly explored hers, his hands did the same to her body, following the curves and contours with gentle, leisurely strokes that made her quiver and sigh.

Then his mouth moved over her jaw, down her throat, across her collarbone. He found her nipple with his tongue, flicked it playfully, then blew gently on the moist peak. She gasped and arched beneath him, silently begging for more.

His hands took over, continuing to tease and caress the aching peaks as his mouth moved lower, his tongue trailing a path down her belly as he nudged her thighs farther apart with his knees.

Her breath caught and her fingers fisted in the sheet as his fingers found the soft curls at her center. Everything inside her was tense, quivering. She wanted him to touch her, but she was already so close to the edge, she knew that if he did, she would fly apart.

"Nate—please. I want you inside me."

"Soon," he said again, then groaned as he slid a finger between the slick folds of skin and into her.

She bit down on her lip to keep from crying out as he withdrew, then sank in again, deeper. When his thumb brushed over her tight, throbbing nub, she could hold back no more. She cried out in shock and pleasure as her body erupted. And still he continued to stroke her, causing wave after wave of sensation to wash over her, the first crashing into the next, relentless and unending.

"Now, Nate. Please."

But instead of giving her what she thought she wanted, he gave her more. His head dipped between her thighs and his mouth settled over her. He nibbled and sucked the tender flesh, his tongue sweeping in and out, quick licks alternating with leisurely strokes that drove her up—high and ever higher.

She wanted to protest, to tell him that he'd already given her so much—too much. But she couldn't find the words. She couldn't even catch her breath. She simply had nothing left, and she knew there was no way—

Oooh.

Her head fell back against the pillows as a kaleidoscope of light and color erupted behind her closed eyelids. Apparently there was a way, and he had found it, and he groaned in appreciation as he tasted her pleasure.

And…*oooh…yesss*.

He gripped her hips in his hands, holding her immobile as he continued his sensual onslaught, as wave after wave of pleasure washed over her and…finally…ebbed.

Then, and only then, did he ease away from her, kissing his way up her body, and finally reach for the condom he'd put on the bedside table. He discarded his briefs, tore open the wrapper and quickly sheathed himself.

Though her heart was still pounding and her skin still tingling, she was aware of the harshness of his breathing, of his eagerness to join his body with hers. She wrapped her arms around him, taking him into her embrace, welcoming him into her body, hoping to give him even a fraction of the pleasure he'd already given her. When he drove into her, the size and strength of him stretched her, filled her, fulfilled her. And—though she would have sworn it was impossible—she came again.

He caught her hands in his, linked them above her head, as he moved inside her. Long, deep strokes that seemed to touch her very center.

"You feel…so…good."

She heard his voice as if from a distance. She blinked, tried to focus, but the world was spinning. She lifted her legs, hooked her ankles together, anchoring herself to him, against the storm of sensations that battered at her from every direction.

His hands slid up her torso, cupped her breasts, his thumbs stroking the peaks of her nipples as he drove into her. She arched up, meeting him thrust for thrust, taking him deeper inside.

She felt connected to him in a way she hadn't experienced in a very long time—if ever before. Their bodies moved and merged together, their breaths—quick and shallow—

mingled and their hearts pounded in synchronized rhythm
as they raced not against but beside each other, and finally
reached...ecstasy.

When Nate returned to the bed after disposing of the condom, Allison was snuggled beneath the sheets, a soft, satisfied smile on her lips. She truly was beautiful, and already,
he wanted her again. He wanted to explore every inch of
her soft, silky skin with his hands and his lips. He wanted
to touch and taste, and drive her as crazy as she drove him
with her soft sighs and breathless gasps.

He'd thought of no one but her since that stolen kiss before Christmas, wanted no one but her. He'd been certain
that *having* would do away with the *wanting* and was surprised again to find it wasn't so. If anything, the first taste
had only whetted his appetite.

He pulled back the sheet and lowered himself onto the
mattress beside her. Her eyelids flickered, opened, and she
offered him a shy smile. "I should probably head back to
my own room."

"Why?"

"So that you can sleep."

"I don't want to sleep." He stroked a hand down her side,
following the feminine dips and curves, and she sighed con-
tentedly. "I don't think I'll ever be able to look at you seated
behind your desk and not remember the way you look right
now."

The pleasure in her eyes dimmed, just a little. "This is
nothing more than a stolen moment," she reminded him.
"Not to be spoken of again after tonight."

"One night," he confirmed, and kissed her softly, gently.
"But the night isn't over yet."

Much to Allison's relief, the storm had cleared up by
morning and the airport was reopened, planes landing and

taking off again as scheduled. Allison wanted to call Dylan, to let him know that she would be home today, but there didn't seem to be any point when she wouldn't see him until the end of the weekend anyway. But she did call the airline, because it had always been part of her job to take care of the travel arrangements and because doing so now was a timely reminder that Nate was the acting CFO of Garrett Furniture and she was his executive assistant. Their brief time as lovers was finished, even if she knew it would never be forgotten.

As she took her seat on the plane, she didn't—couldn't—regret those stolen hours of bliss, which had been so much more than she'd imagined. She hadn't intended to stay through the night, but she'd fallen asleep in his arms and awakened the same way. Though she'd been reluctant to slip from the comfort of his embrace, she'd known it was necessary. But he'd caught her at the edge of the mattress, pulled her back to the center of the bed and shown her the heights and depths of pleasure again.

It had been a long time since she'd been with a man—but she wasn't inexperienced. She'd had several lovers before she'd hooked up with Jeff, but she'd never had a lover like Nathan Garrett.

She didn't think there was anything he didn't do well, and now she could add lovemaking to the list. Of course, she shouldn't be surprised—if even half the rumors that circulated through the break room were to be believed, he'd certainly had enough practice. And somehow he'd turned a physical act into a lovely and breathtaking art.

And now, after only one night, she was turning into a romantic fool. Thankfully, they'd both agreed to the one-night deal. It wouldn't do for her to be caught daydreaming about the boss when she was behind her desk at Garrett Furniture. She needed to get back home, to get her feet back on solid ground, to remember all the reasons that they weren't right for each other—even for the short term.

The plane touched down smoothly, but she felt the jolt of the landing inside her. It was over now. They were back in North Carolina, back to reality. She slung her messenger bag over her shoulder, he picked up his briefcase and they walked out of the airport together.

The air was cold enough that she could see her breath in the air, but the sky was clear, the ground barely dusted with snow. Further proof that they were miles away from St. Louis and the intimacy they'd shared.

But Nate stood close enough that she could feel the heat from his body, and her own stirred with memory, with longing. She took a deliberate step away from him as she dug into her purse for her keys.

"I'm going to send John a text, to let him know that I'm stopping at home for a quick shower and change of clothes before I head into the office."

"I'm going to do the same," he told her.

"Don't forget you have a three o'clock meeting with your uncle and the incoming VP of Finance."

"I won't forget—you programmed the reminders for all of my meetings for the next two weeks into my phone."

"I did." She remembered now, and felt foolish that she'd forgotten. But so much had happened in the past twenty-four hours, so much had changed—not just between them but within her—that she was having trouble finding her footing and clearing her head.

"So…I'll see you at three," he said.

"I'll see you at three," she confirmed.

His smoky eyes held hers for a long minute and he looked as if he wanted to say something more, but in the end, he only nodded and turned away.

It was both unrealistic and naive to think that having sex with a woman wouldn't change things between them.

Nate was neither unrealistic nor naive, and while he knew

that Allison's concerns about their working relationship were valid, he was confident that they could both move forward with their professional relationship.

Some women tended to romanticize sex—wanting to turn the physical act into a meaningful relationship. Thankfully, he didn't have to worry about that with Allison, because she was the one who'd insisted that their one night together wouldn't ever be anything more.

The problem was that when he went to the CFO's office for his meeting and saw her sitting behind her desk, he realized that the one night they'd spent together had done nothing to conquer his desire for her. If anything, he only wanted her more.

As John went over the most recent numbers from their Gallery stores, Nate found his attention continually shifting to the woman outside. She was wearing a different pantsuit now—this one was charcoal gray with a subtle pinstripe. Beneath the jacket she wore something lacy and pink that immediately brought to mind the camisole he'd stripped from her body the night before.

"Any questions?"

Nate forced his attention back to his uncle. "Um, no. I think that covers everything."

"Keep an eye on New York," John suggested. "It might be that we'll want to expand there in the very near future."

He nodded and made a note on the page.

"Of course, Allison will undoubtedly send you a reminder to check in with Seth Overton—the manager there—after the fourth-quarter numbers are in."

He nodded again as his uncle's phone buzzed.

John picked up the receiver. "I know," he said without preamble. "I'm on my way now."

He chuckled as he listened to the response on the other end before hanging up.

"I've got a doctor's appointment," he told Nate. "Allison wanted to make sure I wouldn't be late."

"She keeps track of your personal appointments, too?"

"She keeps track of my life," John said, pushing his chair back from his desk. "Last year, when we were in the midst of that audit in San Francisco, I almost forgot my anniversary. Allison made the arrangements to fly Ellen out to California, had flowers waiting in our hotel room when she arrived, a spa appointment booked and dinner reservations made so that all I had to do was show up at the restaurant."

He took his coat off a hook behind his door. "I honestly don't know what I would have done without her for the past six years. She's not just an asset to this office but an incredible person."

He slid his arms into the sleeves. "Although I'm sure you figured that out for yourself last night."

"What?"

"Last night—when you were stuck in St. Louis," John prompted. "I hope you spent some time getting to know her."

Probably more intimately than his uncle could imagine—definitely more than he would approve.

"We had dinner at the hotel," he said, because that was both a true and safe response. "I found out that she has a kid."

His uncle nodded. "Dylan—a great kid. Although incredibly shy."

"You know him?"

"Sure. Allison usually brings him to the summer picnic. And she would sometimes pick him up from school and bring him back to the office if she was working late on something."

The summer picnic was very much a family thing, which was why Nate had preferred to avoid it if at all possible. And it was usually possible.

The phone on John's desk buzzed again.

He opened the office door. "You nag worse than my wife," he told his executive assistant.

"She was nagging on behalf of your wife," Ellen said to her husband, who looked duly chagrined.

"You didn't have to come over here to go with me," he protested. "It's just a checkup."

"It's the only way I can be sure you don't edit the doctor's instructions when you pass them on to me," his wife said.

John's heavy sigh was confirmation that he did just that. "Have a good weekend, Allison. And you, too, Nate."

Allison smiled as she watched them make their way to the elevator, bickering affectionately all the way.

"They're good together," she noted. "Even after forty-four years, you can tell they still love each other."

"The true test is going to come when Uncle John is at home full-time."

"You're probably right."

"Why are you still here?" he asked. "I thought you usually finished early on Fridays."

"Usually," she agreed. "But Jeff has Dylan for the weekend, so there was no reason for me to rush off."

"You're on your own tonight?" He couldn't help but feel hopeful that her solitary status might allow a repeat of the previous night's activities, despite her explicit statement to the contrary.

"Just me and all the chores that get overlooked day to day."

"That sounds…" He wasn't sure how to finish the thought. Chores definitely didn't sound as interesting as what he'd been thinking, but he couldn't share those thoughts with her now.

She smiled. "Incredibly mundane and boring?"

"Actually, yes," he admitted. While he wasn't a stranger to washing dishes or doing laundry, neither was on his list of plans for a Friday night.

"My life, for the most part, is incredibly mundane and boring."

"Including last night?"

She dropped her gaze as color filled her cheeks. "Last night was definitely...out of the ordinary."

"Extraordinary," he agreed, and the color in her cheeks deepened.

"Did your uncle mention a possible expansion of the Gallery in New York?" she asked, in a deliberate attempt to shift the topic of conversation back to more neutral ground.

He'd obviously flustered her, and he was gratified to know that she wasn't as unaffected by the intimacy they'd shared the night before as she wanted him to believe. Satisfied with that, at least for now, he responded to her question. "He said we should look at it after the final numbers are in for the fourth quarter."

She nodded. "I'll make a note to do that."

But as she shut down her computer, he suspected that she had already done so. She was, as his uncle had said, an asset to the office. He had yet to figure out what other role she might play in his life, but he knew that they weren't finished yet.

Not even close.

Chapter Seven

Most of the time, her life was incredibly mundane and boring, and Allison was okay with that. She liked predictability and routines and quiet nights at home. Okay—she liked steamy-hot sex with a certain corporate executive, too, but the night she'd spent with Nate had been pure fantasy, and it was time for her to focus on reality again. And her reality right now, after having finished the first load of laundry and vacuuming through the apartment, was figuring out a dinner plan.

She'd intended to meet Chelsea at Marg & Rita's, the local Mexican restaurant, but her friend had texted earlier to say she had to work because Ty was off with the flu. Allison considered walking over to the bar to grab a bite and share some conversation with her friend, but she wasn't in the mood for the crowd.

Unfortunately, since grocery shopping was still on the part of her to-do list that was not yet done, she didn't have a lot of options for dinner. There was a pizza in the freezer, and though it didn't look very appealing and she didn't know how long it had actually been in there, she set the oven to preheat.

She was scrolling through the Netflix menu when a knock sounded at the door. Since no one could get into the building without being buzzed through the secure door in the lobby, she assumed it was probably Mrs. Hanson from across the hall.

The old woman liked to bake, but she always seemed to

be in need of a stick of butter or a cup of sugar or a package of semisweet chocolate chips. Allison had learned that keeping those staple ingredients on hand meant she and Dylan would reap the benefits of whatever Mrs. Hanson baked.

Anticipating her elderly neighbor, she was surprised to find Nate standing on the other side of her door.

"Nate. Um, hi." She was suddenly conscious of the fact that she was wearing a pair of yoga pants and an old UNCW T-shirt with her hair pulled back in a haphazard ponytail and her feet bare.

He smiled and offered her the bouquet of flowers in his hand. "Hi."

"Oh." She was touched by the unexpected gesture, and just a little wary. "Thanks."

"My sister-in-law, Rachel, is a florist—Buds and Blooms."

"Not that I have any objection to getting flowers," she said. "But why?"

"Because I wanted an excuse to drop by," he admitted.

"How did you get into the building?"

"An older woman who said she lives across the hall from you," he told her.

"Mrs. Hanson?"

He nodded. "That was her name. As I was looking at the tenant directory, she came through the lobby and asked who the flowers were for. When I mentioned your name, she said that spring flowers always made her think of sunny days and that it was about time you had a devastatingly handsome man bring you flowers and put some sunshine into your life."

She lifted a brow. "Devastatingly handsome?"

He grinned. "I might have embellished a little."

"Well, I guess I should invite you to come in while I find a vase for these."

He followed her into the kitchen. She opened the cupboard above the fridge and pulled out a Waterford crystal

vase—a memento of her long ago and ill-fated wedding—
then filled it with water.

"I heard what you said—about last night being only one
night. I didn't come here expecting to take you to bed but
hoping that I could take you out to dinner."

"Why?"

"Maybe I was hoping dinner with me would be a step up
from mundane and boring," he suggested.

"And it would be," she agreed. "Several steps up, in fact.
But it wouldn't be a good idea."

"Valentino's is always a good idea."

"Until someone we know sees us together, then it's a date
and the hot topic of office gossip."

"I'm sure people have better things to talk about than
my personal life."

"Where do you think I heard about your ski trip with
Lanie?"

"I already told you—it wasn't a ski trip with Lanie, we
just happened to be at the same resort."

"And I believe you," she told him. "But rumor is always
more interesting than truth."

"If you won't go to Valentino's with me—will you let me
bring Valentino's to you?"

Sharing a meal with him in the privacy of her apartment
might protect her reputation, but it could also jeopardize her
heart. Because the more time she spent with him, the more
she saw different facets of his personality, and the more she
realized that she actually liked him. And that was dangerous
because he didn't do relationships and—what happened in
St. Louis notwithstanding—she didn't do flings.

But he looked so earnest and she really wasn't in the
mood for frozen pizza. So instead of sending him away, she
replied, "Only if it's lasagna."

* * *

Half an hour later, he was back with lasagna and garlic bread and a bottle of pinot noir.

They chatted easily while they ate. More easily than she would have expected, considering that only twenty-four hours earlier, they'd been naked and horizontal together. But they kept the conversation fairly neutral.

She was surprised to learn that he'd turned down a baseball scholarship to Stanford because he wanted to go to NYU. It was only when she prompted him for more details about his decision that he admitted his grandmother had been ill at the time and he also didn't want to be too far away from his family. Apparently he'd played second base at Hillfield Academy with fifty-two home runs and a .384 batting average over four years—which were also details she had to pry out of him. Though she didn't know much about baseball, she knew the statistics were impressive. But even more impressive to Allison was that he'd wanted to be part of his family's company more than he'd wanted to pursue the possibility of playing professional ball.

Although they didn't touch on anything too personal, she couldn't deny there was a hum of something in the air. Or maybe it was just that her head was buzzing from the wine, because Nate had limited himself to a single glass so he could keep a clear head to drive home. She half wondered if he made the statement in the hope that she would tell him he could stay, if he expected that the pleasure he'd given to her the night before would entice her to want to repeat it. But though she was undeniably tempted, she said nothing.

She was, after all, the one who had established the ground rules. If she changed her mind now, if she pushed aside the barriers that she'd erected, she couldn't expect him to respect them in the future. On the other hand, he was Nate

Garrett, and the idea that his interest would extend so far in time to anything that might be considered "future" was improbable if not impossible.

In fact, his interest had probably already waned because, aside from showing up at her apartment with flowers and inviting her to dinner, he seemed perfectly content to play by her rules. He hadn't touched her or kissed her or given any indication that he was aching for her the way she was aching for him. And she was, admittedly, more than a little disappointed.

But as they cleared away the dishes in the kitchen, she felt something in the air between them. And when she looked at him, she saw the want in his gaze.

"I guess I should be going."

"That's probably a good idea," she agreed.

He picked up his jacket and made his way to the door. "Thanks for dinner."

"Thanks for not making me eat alone on a Friday night."

"I have no doubt that you would have found someone else to have dinner with if I'd sent you away."

"I didn't want to have dinner with anyone else." He lifted a hand and cupped her cheek. "I don't want anyone else."

She swallowed. "We had an agreement," she said, to remind herself as much as him.

"I wasn't of sound mind when I accepted your terms."

"You weren't of sound mind?"

His thumb traced the curve of her bottom lip. "I was crazy with wanting you."

And he was making her crazy now. He'd barely touched her, but her blood was pulsing, her body quivering.

"I'm not going to have an affair with my boss," she said, though without much conviction.

"I'm not your boss yet," he reminded her.

"You tried that argument once before," she reminded him.

"It's still a valid point."

"What happened last night…I don't do things like that. I'm not spontaneous and impulsive and irresponsible—not anymore. I can't be."

He tipped her chin up, forcing her to meet his gaze. "How about beautiful and sexy and passionate? Because you're definitely all of those, no matter how much you try to deny it."

"And you know just what to say to make me forget all of the reasons I decided that what happened last night couldn't happen again."

"So maybe they weren't very good reasons," he suggested.

"Maybe they weren't," she acknowledged, linking her hand with his. "Are you going to stay?"

"I thought you'd never ask."

It wasn't just a fact but a matter of pride that Nate didn't chase after women. He'd never had to. Since he'd hit puberty, women had chased him and, when the attraction was reciprocated, he happily let himself get caught. But never for the long term.

His mother frequently lamented his penchant for frequent and casual relationships, and although Nate didn't like disappointing her, he had no intention of settling just to make her happy. He enjoyed the company of women, both in and out of bed, but he didn't play fast and loose with their emotions. He was always careful to select women who wanted the same thing he did—a good time.

Allison Caldwell was not his usual type. She was beautiful and sexy and smart—which were all qualities he admired in a woman—but she had a kid, and the whole family thing had never been his scene. Sure, he enjoyed hanging out with *his* family—his parents and brothers and aunts and uncles and cousins—even the little ones. But he had no desire to be part of a core family unit.

He'd let himself forget that when he was with Allison. He

couldn't claim that he didn't know about her son, but when they'd been stranded together in St. Louis, her kid had been more than eight hundred miles away. Of course, she'd given him absolutely no reason to believe that she expected—or even wanted—anything more than what they'd shared that night. He was the one who had stopped by her apartment, unannounced and uninvited. He was the one who'd spent the night with her in a bed less than eight feet across the hall from her son's bedroom. Not that he'd been there—but that wasn't the point.

Actually, he wasn't even sure that there was a point, except that showing up at her apartment—with flowers no less—made him worry that he was chasing her. When they were stranded together, it was easy to blame the circumstances of the storm, the temptation of proximity. But as soon as they got back to North Carolina, that should have been the end of it. She'd told him that would be the end of it.

But he'd been unable to let her go. He'd spent both Friday and Saturday nights with her, in her bed; he'd shared the narrow shower in her en suite bathroom; he'd eaten breakfast at the little bistro table in her kitchen; and even when it was time to head to his parents' house for Sunday night dinner, he hadn't wanted to leave her.

He'd actually, for just a minute, considered inviting her to go with him. And that, he suspected, would have been a disaster of monumental proportions. Not just because everyone knew her as his uncle's executive assistant, but because he hadn't invited a woman to his parents' home in probably ten years.

Thankfully, sanity had reigned and he'd kissed her goodbye and went to Sunday night dinner alone. But that moment of consideration had shaken him. After only a few days and nights, he couldn't seem to get her out of his mind. Which was why, when he found himself with nothing to do the following Saturday night, he called his cousin Ryan and arranged to meet him at O'Reilly's Pub.

But even that choice had been colored by his determination to push all thoughts of Allison out of his mind. Ryan had suggested the Bar Down, but Nate knew that if they went there, chances were good that Chelsea would be working, and seeing Chelsea would make him think about Allison and he was determined not to think about Allison tonight—except that he was only halfway through his first beer and doing a lousy job of controlling his thoughts already.

"This must be my lucky day," Jordyn said, sidling up to the other side of the bar. "Two of my favorite cousins in one place."

"She wants something," Ryan said to Nate.

He nodded. "The question is—what?"

"*I* don't want anything," Jordyn assured them. "But I know Lauryn would really appreciate some help putting up the shelves she bought for the baby's room."

"Shouldn't her husband be able to do that?" Ryan asked.

"You'd think so. Unfortunately, Rob doesn't seem to know the difference between a hammer and a drill." Jordyn's disgusted tone left them in no doubt about her feelings toward her sister's husband.

"Which doesn't mean that she'd be willing to accept our help," Nate pointed out.

Because Lauryn hated that everyone knew Rob had taken the money her parents gave them for a down payment on a house and used it instead to prop up his failing business. Especially when, three years later, the business was still on shaky ground.

Nate always thought it was both a blessing and a curse to be part of a large, close-knit family. The blessing was that there was always someone ready to lend a hand when it was needed; the curse was that there was no way to hide the fact that it was needed. Lauryn and Rob had gone through some rough patches in their marriage recently, and when Lauryn had called everyone together at the end of the previous summer, there was speculation within the family that they might call it quits. Instead, she'd announced that she was pregnant.

With a baby on the way, Lauryn had been determined to move out of their apartment and into a house—and she refused to take any more money from her family. They used their limited funds to purchase a fixer-upper that Rob promised to fix up for their new family, but it was still in rough shape and mortgaged to the hilt.

"She keeps insisting that Rob will get around to doing the things she wants done," Jordyn told them, "but I know that if he doesn't do them soon, she will. And I don't think, at seven and a half months pregnant, she should be climbing a ladder."

Ryan frowned. "She wouldn't."

Nate didn't like to think so, but he had to disagree with his cousin. "She would."

Jordyn nodded.

He sighed. "When?"

"Tomorrow would be great."

"I'm not doing anything," Nate confirmed.

"I'm going to be out of town," Ryan said.

"Convenient," Jordyn said.

"No, really, there's a thing I have to go to in Winston-Salem."

"I'll snag Andrew to help," Nate decided. "He's the carpenter."

"Thank you." Jordyn poured another draft, set it in front of him. "Sincerely."

He just nodded.

"What about me?" Ryan lifted his half-empty glass.

She put another under the tap, filled it. "His is on the house—you're paying for yours," she said. "And don't forget to tip your server."

Nate waited until Jordyn had moved down the bar to serve another customer before he turned to his cousin. "A thing in Winston-Salem? What kind of thing?"

"The baptism," Ryan admitted. "My friends Darren and Melissa's little guy."

"That's right," Nate suddenly remembered. "You're going to be the godfather."

His cousin nodded.

"Does it freak you out?"

"Why would it?"

Nate shrugged. "I don't know—the whole idea of being responsible for someone else's kid seems pretty scary to me."

"It's not like I really have to do anything other than sign my name to a piece of paper," Ryan said.

"And smile for pictures."

"Yeah, that might be a challenge."

"Why do you say that?"

"Because Harper Ross is going to be Oliver's godmother."

"The maid of honor?"

Ryan nodded again.

"I thought you liked her."

"No, I said she was hot."

"My mistake." Nate picked up his beer again and settled back to watch the game.

On the thirtieth of January, there was a big party in the office for John Garrett. Allison had taken care of all the details: streamers and balloons, the banner proclaiming Congratulations on Your Retirement, the enormous sheet cake and bowls of punch and urns of coffee.

It was the end of an era for Garrett Furniture, and she was feeling a little nostalgic as she wandered around the now-empty office. She really was going to miss seeing John on a daily basis. On a more positive note, she felt pretty good about working with his nephew. Over the past couple of weeks, she'd sat in on numerous meetings with Nate and had countless conversations with him, and had managed—mostly—to stay focused. It was almost as if those few nights they'd spent together had never happened.

But when she was alone in her bed, she couldn't help but remember those nights that she hadn't been alone. It wasn't just that her body ached for his touch; she found that she actually missed his company. Maybe it was a sign that she was ready to start dating again. Now that Dylan was older and more independent, maybe it was time to find someone to share her life. Except that when she thought about dating, she couldn't help thinking about the awkward getting-to-know-someone moments, and she didn't miss those at all.

As she made her way around the office, looking for empty cups and forgotten plates, she tried not to think about the fact that this would be her last time tidying up John's office, because it was now Nate's office. And she tried not to wonder where her new boss had gone. He'd been there for the party, of course, but he'd slipped out to take a phone call. Less than a minute later, Melanie had followed.

She believed that nothing had happened between them in Vail. Certainly he had no reason to lie to her about the fact. It was equally evident that the other woman was hoping to rectify that situation. Allison didn't blame her—Nate Garrett was, by all accounts, quite a catch. The only problem, as she saw it, was that he had no intention of ever being caught.

She didn't regret the time they'd spent together, but it was hard not to wish there had been more of it. Her choice, she knew, and the right decision. She didn't ever want to be like Melanie, chasing after a guy who clearly didn't want the same things she did.

She was almost finished tidying up in the CFO's office when Nate returned.

"We do have a cleaning service, you know," he said to her.

"I know," she confirmed. "I'm just giving them a hand."

"I'm starting to realize that you do a lot more around here than I ever suspected."

She shrugged. "My job description is pretty vague."

"Does it including putting up nameplates?" He gestured to the engraved brass on the door.

"I put it up," she acknowledged. "But it was your uncle's idea."

"It's a nice touch," he said. He moved a little closer. He didn't touch her, but he was near enough that she could feel the warmth of his breath on her cheek, and her own caught in her throat.

"I've missed you."

"You've seen me almost every day."

"You know what I mean," he chided.

She nodded, because she did. "But we both knew it was going to be like this."

"It's funny," he said. "I've been waiting for my uncle to retire for more than two years. Now that it's finally happened, I can't help wishing he'd stayed on another six months so that we could have had that time to figure out what's between us and where to go from here."

"Six months wouldn't make any difference," she told him. "We'd still end up exactly where we are now."

"How do you know?"

"Because you don't do serious and I don't do casual."

"But we both have to eat," he pointed out.

"Most people do," she agreed.

"I know you would have left two hours ago if your son wasn't with his dad this weekend, so why don't you come back to my place for dinner tonight?"

She shook her head regretfully. "I appreciate the offer, but I can't."

"Okay, we'll skip dinner and go straight to sex."

She managed a laugh. "Tempting, but no."

"C'mon, Alli. Meet me halfway."

"Halfway to what?"

Before he could respond, Melanie peeked around the door. "There you are," she said to Nate. "I've been looking all over for you."

The teasing glint in his eyes faded; his expression grew wary. "Is there a problem?" he asked.

"Of course not—I just wanted you to know that a bunch of us are heading over to Tonic to continue the party."

Nate lifted his brows at the mention of the trendy dance club that was popular with the twenty-something crowd. "My uncle's going to Tonic?"

Melanie giggled. "No—this party is for the new CFO."

"Oh. Well. That's very kind but—"

"Don't say you can't come to your own party," Melanie admonished.

He looked helplessly toward Allison. "Will you come, too?"

"I can't," she said. "But I'm sure you'll have a great time."

Nate looked disappointed by her response, but she refused to feel guilty that she'd abandoned him to the company of an obviously willing woman. Instead, she turned and exited the CFO's office, not wanting to hear the rest of their conversation.

If Nate truly had missed Allison, she had no doubt that Melanie would ensure he didn't continue to miss her for long. And maybe that was for the best.

Chapter Eight

From the moment Nate took over the corner office, he was a consummate professional and perfectly circumspect in his behavior toward Allison. She was the one who couldn't seem to stop thinking about the fact that she'd been naked with him. But she was confident that the memories—and the longing—would fade in time.

He made a three-day trip to Austin in early February. He asked her if she wanted to go with him, but didn't push when she said that she couldn't. She wasn't sure if she was relieved or disappointed, but she knew it was for the best. Her job was much more important than her tumultuous feelings for her boss—a fact of which she was clearly reminded when she got called to the school because Dylan was having an asthma attack.

It turned out not to be serious. In fact, by the time she arrived, he'd treated himself with the rescue inhaler he carried in his backpack, but the episode terrified her—as such episodes always did. Thankfully, her son's attacks were now fewer and further between than they'd been a few years back, but they always made her take stock of what was most important in life—and the answer was always Dylan.

Of course, Chelsea was fond of pointing out that Dylan wouldn't always be a little boy, that someday he would go off to school and a life of his own, leaving Allison alone. She was prepared for that—but she wasn't prepared to ever let her son feel as if he wasn't the most important person in her life, especially since he knew his place in the hierarchy of his father's family and it wasn't at the top.

Sure, there were times that she wondered if she might ever be anything more than a mother—when she thought about how she'd felt in Nate's arms and wished she could reconcile her responsibilities and her desires. But for all she knew, Nate had already lost interest in her. Sometimes when she was working, she'd glance into his office and find him looking back at her, but she was never able to interpret what those looks meant. Or maybe she just unwilling to let herself hope.

Nate might not have realized it was Valentine's Day if not for the enormous bouquet of flowers on Alli's desk. But he couldn't even glance into the outer office without seeing the colorful blooms that spilled out of the tall frosted-glass vase beside her computer monitor. They'd been delivered early that morning—a beautiful and elaborate arrangement of orange and pink gerberas mixed with red carnations and purple alstroemeria (and he admittedly only knew what that was because he'd asked Rachel when he saw it in her wedding bouquet). There was a card peeking out of the top of the arrangement, but he wasn't able to get close enough to see it without making it obvious that he was looking.

He didn't care—he *shouldn't* care. It wasn't any of his business who was sending her flowers. Allison was no longer his uncle's executive assistant, but his own, and she'd made it clear that she wasn't going to get involved with her boss. But he didn't like to think that she was involved with anyone else, either. She hadn't mentioned that she was seeing anyone, but she wouldn't. She didn't talk about her personal life. Ordinarily, he would appreciate that kind of discretion, but now, wanting to know the identity of the man who had sent her Valentine's Day flowers was driving him to distraction.

And what if he did see the name on the card? What if the card was signed "All my love, Gunther"? He didn't know any Gunthers, but it was a pretty fair bet that he wouldn't be able to track the guy down on the basis of his name. And even if he could, what was he going to do about it? Show up at his door and beat him up because he had the right to send a bouquet to Allison and Nate didn't? Besides, he didn't want to send her flowers. Flowers—especially Valentine's Day flowers—implied a relationship they didn't have.

He'd given her flowers once—a simple bouquet of spring flowers because she'd told him that was what she liked. Either the sender of this arrangement didn't really know her taste or was determined to make a statement about their relationship.

Just because they'd spent one weekend together four weeks earlier didn't give him any proprietary claim, and just because he wasn't seeing anyone else didn't mean that she couldn't be. But the possibility did not sit well with him.

He went to her desk to pick up the latest sales reports from San Diego.

"I was going to bring those in to you before your conference call," she told him.

"I didn't realize you were even there," he lied. "I couldn't see you past the flower shop on your desk."

Her cheeks colored as she glanced at the bouquet. "A little over the top, isn't it?"

"It definitely tips the scales on the opposite side of subtle," he acknowledged. Then, in a deliberately casual move, he shifted so that he could read the message buried in the flowers.

Thinking about you—today and always! Love, C.

"Who's C?"

She glanced up. "Sorry?"

He gestured to the card. "Who's C?" he asked again.

"Oh." The color in her cheeks deepened as she shook her head. "A friend."

"Those flowers make a pretty strong statement from a... friend."

"No doubt that was the intention. Everyone who saw the delivery arrive has been whispering and wondering," she told him. "So far speculation has ranged from Cody in service to Chad in HR to Carter in marketing."

"Apparently no one is aware of your refusal to date someone you work with," he mused.

"It could be argued that I don't really work with Cody, since our paths have never crossed during the workday."

"Are you saying that they are from Cody?"

She shook her head. "I was only making the point that I don't work with Cody. In fact, I don't even know him."

"So who are they from?" he pressed.

"Chelsea," she finally admitted.

"Chelsea Lawrence?"

She nodded. "It started several years ago, when she broke up with her boyfriend only a few days before Valentine's Day. She was more upset than the breakup warranted and finally confessed that she just wanted to have one Valentine's Day that she didn't spend alone.

"It can be a difficult day for single women—so I sent flowers to cheer her up. The next year, I did the same, and so did she. Since then, it's become a tradition."

"Even when she was in a relationship, a couple of years ago, she told her boyfriend that she couldn't go out with him on Valentine's Day, because she had plans to hang out with me."

"Is that what you're doing tonight—hanging out with Chelsea?"

"Yep. With pizza and wings from Valentino's and a pitcher of Chelsea's trademark sangria." Her fingers continued to move efficiently over the keyboard as she spoke. "What are your plans?"

He shook his head. "I have none."

She seemed surprised by that. "You don't have a date on Valentine's Day?"

"Not unless you invite me to share your pizza and wings."

"Sorry," she said, not sounding sorry at all. "Girls only."

"What about your son?"

"Dylan's with his dad this weekend," she said, then glanced down as a reminder chimed from her computer. "You've got that conference call in fifteen minutes."

He nodded, grateful for the reminder and the redirection. She'd told him, and more than once, that their interlude together was over. If he thought it had been far too brief, apparently he was the only one. By all appearances, she was content in her role as his executive assistant and didn't want anything more.

He couldn't deny that he still wanted her—but he'd be damned before he'd beg. He took the file back to his office to prep for his conference call.

Since Valentino's was between Chelsea's town house and Allison's apartment, Chelsea picked up the pizza and wings on the way. Allison put the food in the oven to keep it warm while Chelsea made the sangria.

Her friend seemed preoccupied with her thoughts while she worked, making Allison wonder if she was unhappy to be spending yet another Valentine's Day with her best friend rather than a romantic liaison. She put out a tray of veggies and dip that she'd prepared earlier and nibbled on a carrot stick.

"Something unusual happened when I went to pick up your order at Valentino's," Chelsea said, as she poured the wine into two glasses.

"Marco flirted with you," Allison guessed.

"Marco flirts with every female who crosses his path—that's not unusual."

"True," she acknowledged. "So what was the something unusual?"

"The pizza and wings had already been paid for."

Allison paused with a cucumber slice in the dip. "What?"

"That was my reaction, too," her friend admitted. "But Gemma said that someone had come in and specifically asked if there was an order for Allison Caldwell. She was worried that she'd misunderstood what time it was supposed to be ready and told him that the pizza was still in the oven—he said he wasn't there to pick it up, just to pay for it."

"That is strange." She popped the cucumber into her mouth.

"So who knew that you were having pizza and wings from Valentino's tonight?" Chelsea asked.

"I mentioned it at the office," she admitted.

"To anyone in particular?"

"It was just a passing comment—I didn't think he was even paying attention."

"Nate Garrett," her friend guessed.

She nodded and picked up her sangria.

"And the plot thickens."

"There is no plot—nothing to thicken."

"You kissed him at Christmas and he bought you dinner on Valentine's Day," Chelsea noted. "It makes me wonder what might have happened in between that you haven't told me."

She sipped her drink. "Mmm—this is fabulous sangria."

"Come on, Alli. I know when you're holding out on me."

"And I only hold out on you when I know you're going to make a big deal out of something that isn't."

"*What* isn't a big deal?" Chelsea demanded.

"Sex in a St. Louis hotel room."

Her friend choked on a cherry tomato.

Allison thumped her on the back.

Chelsea held up a hand to ward her off as she lifted her glass and swallowed a mouthful of sangria. "For real?"

She nodded, then gestured to the DVDs she'd selected from her collection. "What's it going to be tonight—*The War of the Roses*, *The Break-Up* or *Thelma & Louise*?"

"Forget the movie," Chelsea said. "I want details about St. Louis."

"It wasn't a big deal," she said pointedly. "It was attraction fueled by proximity and a very nice cabernet."

Her friend frowned. "That's it? That's all the detail you're going to give me?"

"And cheesecake." Allison took the pizza and wings out of the oven. "There was this incredible cheesecake with strawberry-Grand Marnier topping."

"A true friend shares details about getting naked with a hot, sexy guy like Nathan Garrett when she knows that her BFF isn't getting any," Chelsea admonished.

"I'm not getting any anymore, either," Allison said.

"It was just that one night?"

She took her time transferring a slice of pizza to her plate, then added five wings. "One weekend," she admitted.

"He slept with you and then he dumped you?"

"There was no dumping to be done—we both agreed at the outset that we weren't going to get involved."

"Why not?"

"Because he's the CFO and I'm his assistant and we both have to focus on doing our jobs. Because Nate Garrett isn't the daddy type and I have an almost-nine-year-old son who is the center of my world."

"He'd love Dylan if he ever had the chance to meet him."

"Not going to happen."

Chelsea sighed, obviously disappointed. "I felt the sizzle between you when you were both at Bar Down. I was sure he was the one for you."

"Even if I were looking for a relationship—which I am *not*—I would not look in Nate Garrett's direction."

"He does have a reputation for being difficult to pin down," her friend agreed. "And yet..."

Allison refused to take the bait, biting into her pizza instead.

"And yet," Chelsea continued, "he went out of his way to buy you dinner on Valentine's Day."

"You can't know that he went out of his way," she argued. "More likely he stopped at Valentino's to pick up something for himself, remembered that I'd mentioned our plans for tonight, and decided that paying for our pizza would be a nice gesture from a boss to his employee."

Chelsea considered that possibility as she nibbled on a chicken wing. "What did he think about the flowers?"

"He said that he hoped Chad and I would be very happy together."

Her friend frowned. "Who's Chad?"

"He works in HR and was widely speculated to be the 'C' who signed the card."

"And Nathan won't go out with you but he's okay with you fraternizing with some guy in HR?"

Allison picked up the pitcher of sangria to refill their glasses. "Actually, I told him that the flowers were from you."

"Why?"

"Because he asked."

"Aha!"

"There's no 'aha.'"

"But there could be," Chelsea insisted.

She shook her head. "I'm not going to jeopardize my employment—and my employee benefits—for a temporary relationship with a guy who isn't capable of anything more."

"How do you know he isn't capable of anything more?"

"The guy is a serial dater."

"I'm not so sure," her friend said. "A true serial dater lives for the chase, and as soon as he gets a woman into his bed, he's ready to move on."

"Exactly," Allison agreed.

"Except that it doesn't sound to me as if he's moved on. In fact, the last time he was in the bar with his brother and Josh Slater, I saw a woman slip him a cocktail napkin with her name and phone number on it—and he crumpled it up and dumped it in the trash."

"Obviously he's a changed man."

Chelsea scowled at the sarcasm. "So what's the office gossip these days?"

"I haven't heard much of anything," she admitted. "But people might be more careful about what they say around me now because they know that he's my boss."

"Or maybe there isn't anything to say." Her friend nibbled on a wing. "You should call him."

"Why?"

"To thank him for dinner."

Allison knew she was right. And if it had been anyone but Nate, she wouldn't have needed her friend to remind her. But initiating contact with her boss, on a weekend, to discuss something that had nothing to do with work, seemed to cross that line she didn't want to cross. "Maybe," she finally said. "But not tonight."

"Why not?"

"Because this is supposed to be our anti-Valentine's Day celebration and men are not invited or discussed, so drink up your sangria and pick a movie."

Chelsea lifted her glass. "Okay, but I have one more thing to say first."

"What's that?" she asked warily.

"I think he could be good for you—and Dylan—if you gave him a chance."

Allison randomly picked a DVD. "*The War of the Roses* then."

Chelsea made a face. "That movie is so depressing. Let's go with *Thelma & Louise*."

"Yeah, because that one has a happy ending," she said drily.

"Maybe it's not happy," her friend acknowledged. "But at least they're together in the end."

"We're going to need another pitcher of sangria, Thelma."

"I'll take care of that, Louise, while you set up the movie."

Nate was scrambling eggs the next morning when his cell phone beeped to announce a text message.

Thanks for dinner.

And reading those three words, his mood lifted.

Usually when a woman says those words to me in the morning, it isn't via text message.

No doubt—apologies if I've interrupted your "morning."

No interruption. I was just making breakfast. As if on cue, the bread popped up out of the toaster.

Breakfast? It's almost lunchtime—she's probably starving by now.

He responded to her message: Okay—we'll call it brunch. But there's no one else here...unless you want to join me?

I don't think so.

He chuckled at the predictable response, could almost

hear the prim tone of her voice as he read the words on the screen. I thought maybe you mentioned dinner as a prelude to another meal.

No, I just mentioned it to say thanks.

He scraped the eggs out of the pan and onto his plate. Before he could reply, she sent another message.

Actually, I wasn't sure if I should text you.

Why not?

Because I only have access to this number because we work together.

So? He poured hot sauce onto his eggs and lifted a forkful to his mouth.

So I wasn't sure if it was inappropriate conduct.

I don't feel as if I'm being stalked...but I haven't completely given up hope.

LOL

He shoveled in another forkful of eggs, because his mother had never reprimanded him about texting with food in his mouth. Do you want my address?

NO!

He chuckled again. Since you're not having brunch with me, how about dinner?

No thanks.

Movie? He bit into a piece of bacon.

No thanks.

A polite brush-off is still a brush-off.

Agreed.

He finished off the eggs, typing awkwardly with one thumb. That sound you can't hear is my ego deflating.

I don't think I can be held responsible for any shrinkage.

Hey!

She didn't respond to that, and he could picture her staring at her phone, her teeth sinking into her bottom lip as she wondered if she'd crossed a line with her response. And though he was admittedly just a bit worried about pushing her beyond her comfort zone, he couldn't resist teasing her a little: Are you…sexting me?

Her response this time was immediate and definite: NO!

Because it sounded like sexual innuendo to me.

It wasn't. Or not intentional, anyway.

Accidental sexual innuendo?

I'm going to do my grocery shopping now.

Is cheesecake on your list? ;)

GOODBYE, Nate.

He let her have the last word, confident that she was at least thinking about him. As he was thinking about her as he finished up his breakfast and put his dishes in the dishwasher.

She was beautiful and sexy and smart and funny. He appreciated that she had her own thoughts and ideas and wasn't afraid to share them. A lot of the women he'd dated seemed to think they needed to echo his opinions or share his interests—which frequently made for boring conversations. He was never bored with Allison.

He hadn't yet figured out how he felt about dating a woman with a child—of course, Allison would be the first to say that they weren't dating. But he wasn't ready to give up on the possibility that they might get there.

When Jeff brought Dylan home the following Wednesday night, Allison decided it was a good opportunity to discuss their son's upcoming birthday.

Jeff, always impatient, glanced at his watch. "I'm well aware that Dylan's birthday is in less than three weeks."

She ignored his defensive tone. "Do you know what you're planning to get for him?"

"What does he want?"

"A Ren D'Alesio jacket and a video game—in that order. I thought I'd give you first choice."

"D'Alesio?" he scowled. "I thought he was a Rayburn fan."

"No—you're the Rayburn fan," she reminded him. "Dylan has always liked D'Alesio, and he's been bugging me about the jacket since he found it online before Christmas."

"Fine—I'll get the jacket."

"You'll have to order it. It's not something you'll be able to pick up the day of his birthday."

"I said I'll get the jacket," he repeated.

And for Dylan's sake, she had to trust that he would.

"Was there anything else?"

She shook her head. "I'll see you next Wednesday."

"That reminds me—I'll probably be a little late bringing him home next week."

"You know I like him to keep to a schedule on school nights."

"I know, but Jillian has a recital in Southern Pines, and the program doesn't finish until eight and then it's an hour-and-a-half drive home again."

"You're going to make Dylan spend his time with you watching a bunch of five-year-olds dance?"

"One of those five-year-olds is his sister."

"Half-sister," she shot back, and immediately felt petty for making the distinction.

"If he doesn't want to come, he doesn't have to come," Jeff told her. "But I'm not missing my daughter's performance."

She noticed that he didn't offer to switch his scheduled visit with his son so that he could attend Jillian's recital but also spend some quality time with Dylan. No, he'd rather sacrifice his time with Dylan than reschedule it, and she couldn't help but feel frustrated on her son's behalf.

"I'll ask Dylan what he wants to do and let you know."

Over the next couple of weeks, Nate proved that he knew how to keep business separate from pleasure. During office hours, he never said or did anything that crossed the lines of their employer-employee relationship. But occasionally, in the evenings, he would send her quick text messages, not usually about anything specific but that would inevitably result in the exchange of a dozen more messages before they signed off.

She didn't think he was seeing anyone—she didn't know

when he would have the time. Since moving into the CFO's office, he'd taken his increased responsibilities seriously and was usually the first to arrive and the last to leave each day. On the last Friday in February, she planned to work late since Dylan was being picked up from school by his father and spending the weekend with him. But shortly after lunch, she started to feel unwell and skipped out early.

By the time she arrived home, she was so cold her teeth were practically chattering. She changed into a pair of yoga pants and a heavy sweater, pulled wool socks onto her feet, and climbed into bed with a cup of herbal tea. She only made it halfway through the drink before fatigue won out and she fell asleep.

She awoke, several hours later, when her cell phone chimed to indicate a text message.

Surprise! Night off, Chelsea texted. *Do you want to catch a movie?*

Sorry—already in bed, Allison typed back, her cold fingers fumbling over the keypad.

With…?

She couldn't even summon the energy to smile in response to her friend's question. *It's actually a threesome: chills, headache, nausea.*

You are sick—3 + U is a 4some.

YOU are sick, I'm ill.

Poor you! Can I bring you anything?

Just want to sleep.

Feel better soon! XO

Allison put the phone down on her bedside table, pulled the covers up to her chin and slept.

She was up several times in the night to race to the bathroom, but even when the meager contents of her stomach had been expelled, the nausea didn't subside. Since she hated dry-heaving more than she hated throwing up, she forced herself to sip on a can of ginger ale and nibble on a few saltine crackers.

She slept late and didn't awaken until she heard footsteps in the hall. Vaguely she remembered texting Chelsea and asking if she could pick up some chicken soup for her, because during one of her late-night forays into the kitchen, she'd discovered that there was none in the pantry.

But it wasn't Chelsea who came through the doorway into her bedroom—it was Nate.

Chapter Nine

She sat up, clutching the covers to her chest. "What are you doing here?"

"You texted me."

"I did not."

"You said that you wanted chicken soup." He held up the plastic container in his hand. "Chicken soup."

She closed her eyes on a moan. "I thought I was texting Chelsea."

"I figured." He put the soup on her bedside table, beside the thermometer and empty ginger ale can. "When was the last time you took your temperature?"

She pushed her hair away from her face. "Sometime last night."

"What was it?"

"One-oh-two."

He touched the back of his hand to her forehead. "You still feel warm."

She pulled away from his touch. "And sweaty. I think I should have a shower before I have that soup."

"Can you manage on your own?"

"You're not really offering to help me?"

He chuckled softly. "I could ask Mrs. Hanson to come over and give you a hand."

"Did she let you into the building again?"

"Yeah, I buzzed her because I didn't want to disturb you

if you were sleeping. She said she suspected you might be sick when you came home from work early yesterday."

Allison sighed. "Who needs a security system when there's Mrs. Hanson across the hall?"

"So do you want some help with that shower?"

"I think I can manage."

"Leave the door unlocked," he suggested. "I don't want to have to break it down if you fall over in the tub."

"I'm not going to fall over," she said, but she appreciated his consideration. If he truly was being considerate and didn't think he could use an unlocked door as an opportunity to peek at her while she was in the shower.

An idea that didn't seem completely out of the realm of possibility until she got a look at herself in the mirror and actually let out a shriek. The startled sound was still hanging in the air when Nate pushed through the door.

"What is it? What happened?"

She shook her head, and reached for the counter when the ground tilted beneath her feet. "Nothing."

He took a step closer, obviously concerned. "Then why did you scream?"

She felt ridiculous admitting the truth to him—and ridiculously vain. But she took it as a positive sign that she actually cared about her appearance today. Twenty-four hours earlier, she'd just wanted to curl up in a ball and pull the blankets over her head.

"Alli?" he prompted.

"I looked in the mirror," she finally confessed.

Somehow, he managed a smile. "It's not one of your best days," he acknowledged, "but you really don't look that bad."

"Am I dying?"

"What?"

"It's the only reason I can think of to explain why you're being so nice to me."

"Maybe I'm a nice guy."

"Maybe you are," she allowed.

"Are you still planning to take a shower?"

"I think we'll both feel better if I do."

"Just give a shout if you want me to wash your back."

She shoved him toward the door.

Upon receipt of Alli's text message asking for chicken soup, Nate had immediately realized that she'd sent it to him in error.

He could have called Chelsea and told her about the message. Probably that's what he should have done. He wasn't the nurturing type. Generally if someone he knew was sick, he kept his distance. He certainly didn't volunteer to play nursemaid. Playing doctor, on the other hand, might be something he could get into, but he knew Allison wasn't in any condition for those kinds of games right now.

But for some reason, her message had compelled him to stop by his parents' house and finagle a container of the homemade chicken soup that his mother always had in the freezer. Of course, asking his mother for the soup gave her an opening to ask questions of her own but, to his surprise, she didn't.

She'd done the same thing countless times when he'd been growing up. If he came home after curfew or she smelled beer on his breath, she never asked any questions—she just gave him that steady, patient stare that always led to him spilling his guts. Which was how he found himself telling her that he was taking the soup to Alli. If she was surprised that he'd make such an overture to a woman who was supposedly nothing more than his executive assistant, she didn't show it. All she said was that she hoped Alli was feeling better soon.

He poured the soup into a pot, then set it on the stove on low, to keep it warm until Allison was ready to eat it. He figured that was his good deed done and should score him some points for when she was feeling better. For now, he'd just wait until she was out of the shower and had eaten some soup, then he could tuck her back into her bed and be on his way. But he knew from experience being sick that it always felt better to stretch out on clean sheets.

No—he wasn't going to do it. Changing the sheets on her bed was too much of a domestic chore. He wasn't her boyfriend. They weren't even sleeping together anymore. Yeah, he hoped that might change, but if not, that was okay. There were plenty of other women around—even if he hadn't wanted any other women since he'd first kissed Allison. Because the realization made him uneasy, he shoved it aside.

Then he heard her coughing. Even though the closed bathroom door and over the sound of the running water, the harsh hacking sound made him cringe in sympathy. Sighing with resignation, he opened the door to what he guessed was the linen closet.

The shower shut off as he was plumping the pillows on her freshly made bed. He heard her moving around in the bathroom and tried not to think about her toweling off her wet and naked body, her silky skin glistening with moisture. When the hair dryer started up, he headed back to the kitchen to check on her soup.

She tracked him down a few minutes later. She'd dressed in a long-sleeved thermal-style shirt and a pair of plaid flannel pajama pants. Her hair, now dry, was tied back in a loose ponytail; her face was bare of makeup and pale except for the dark shadows beneath her eyes. She wouldn't win any beauty contests today, so why did he feel a tug in the vicinity of his heart? What was it about this woman that appealed to him on a level he'd never before experienced? And why did his fascination intrigue him as much as it terrified him?

Allison was wary about the soup.

It looked and smelled delicious, but the experience of the

past twenty-four hours warned her that whatever she put in her stomach might come back up again.

She sipped carefully from the spoon. The first tentative taste went down easily, so she followed it with a second. Before she knew it, the small bowl was empty.

"Feeling better now?" Nate asked.

She nodded.

"You look better."

She managed a wry smile. "I don't think it was possible to look any worse."

"The shower helped," he agreed. "But you've also got a little bit of color back in your cheeks since you ate."

"The soup was delicious."

"My mom's secret recipe."

"I'll do my best to keep it down," she promised.

And while it had felt good to sit at the table to eat, that effort had zapped the last of her energy. She pushed back her chair to carry her bowl and spoon to the sink, but he took them from her and set them down again.

"I'll take care of that when you're in bed," he told her.

Too tired to protest, she let him guide her back to the bedroom. He pulled back the covers and she lowered herself onto the mattress covered in a crisp pale blue sheet.

"You changed the sheets," she realized.

"I thought you'd sleep better in a fresh bed."

He'd brought her soup; he'd changed her sheets. He'd done more to take care of her in the space of two hours than her ex-husband had done in more than two years of marriage. The realization that this man—her boss and former lover—could show such compassion and consideration brought tears to her eyes.

When the first one slid down her cheek, Nate took an instinctive step back. "I can change them back," he offered.

She managed to choke out a laugh as she shook her head.

"I don't want them changed back. I just don't understand... why are you doing this?"

"Has no one ever taken care of you?"

"Not in a very long time," she admitted.

He pulled the covers up to her chin, as she still did for Dylan every night that he slept at home.

"Thank you," she said. "For everything."

"My pleasure."

She might have smiled at that, but she was too busy fighting against a yawn.

"Sleep now," he said, and touched his lips to her forehead. "I'll be here if you need anything."

"You don't have to stay."

"Maybe I want to."

"It's a Saturday night."

"Yes, it is," he confirmed.

"You must have something better to do on a Saturday night."

"Actually, I don't."

Her eyelids felt heavy, and she didn't have the strength to hold them open anymore. "I'm not going to have sex with you."

"Not tonight," he agreed.

But she didn't hear his response—she was already asleep.

Something changed between them that weekend.

Even more than after the weekend they'd spent together in her bed, their relationship shifted. There was another element now—a closeness and trust that hadn't been there before.

Allison stayed home from work on Monday, but Nathan texted her periodically throughout the day to make sure she was eating/drinking/resting. She went back to the office on Tuesday, and Nate left for Miami a few hours later.

She was thinking about him as she opened the mail that

afternoon. It was methodical work—slitting through the tops of the envelopes, sorting the contents into piles, tossing the junk into the trash. She didn't pay any attention to how they were addressed—not until she came across an envelope for John Garrett that was marked "Personal and Confidential."

A few similar envelopes had come across her desk before, but she hadn't seen one in more than a year, at least. Possibly two.

"Personal and Confidential" meant none of her business, and she set it aside to deliver to John at the earliest opportunity.

But she couldn't help wondering who was sending the letters. The handwriting on the envelope was undeniably feminine. She'd worked for the man for six years. She'd spent a lot of time with him and his family—his wife and their three sons—and she'd always noted how completely and utterly devoted he was to Ellen. It wasn't possible that he'd cheated on her. Allison didn't—couldn't—believe it.

She jolted when the phone rang, and her heart started to pound when she saw that it was her direct line. Probably Nate—which was just one more dilemma to add to her day. Should she tell him about the letter?

Her instinctive response was "no." It wasn't her place to tell him anything—especially when she didn't know for sure that there was anything to tell. But she'd never been very good at keeping secrets, so she tried to convince herself that she was reading too much into the feminine handwriting on an envelope addressed to his uncle.

She stuffed the letter into her purse to deliver to John at the earliest opportunity. Then she reached for the phone, but the call had already gone to voice mail.

Dylan's actual birthday was on Friday, but since it wasn't his weekend with his dad, Jeff promised that they would celebrate on the Wednesday before.

But at 2:33 p.m. on that day, Allison got a text message from her ex-husband saying that he was tied up at work and asking if she could get their son.

Dylan was surprised and—she could tell—a little disappointed by the change of plans, but he dutifully did his homework while he waited for his dad to show up. He was on his last page when Jeff finally buzzed up from the lobby.

"He's just finishing up his math, but he's ready to go," Allison told her ex-husband when he showed up at the door.

"Actually, we're not going anywhere."

"What are you talking about?"

He blew out a breath. "I have to cancel our plans for tonight."

She mentally counted to ten—in Spanish, because it required more thought and gave her a few extra seconds to try to control her reaction to his announcement. "You're canceling your plans to celebrate Dylan's birthday?"

"I have to."

"But you promised to take him to Buster Bear's." Not that the popular children's party location had been Dylan's choice, but she knew he'd been looking forward to celebrating with his dad.

"Because Jodie and I were going to take the whole family," Jeff explained, "but the girls both have the flu."

"So why can't you and Dylan go?"

"Because Jodie's pulling her hair out trying to deal with two sick kids and a baby."

"Dylan's going to be nine," she pointed out. "There aren't going to be many more years that he even wants to spend his birthday with either of us."

"I feel awful about this, but I don't have a choice. I did bring his gift, though," he said, and handed her a flat wrapped package.

A package that looked distressingly similar to another

one that she'd wrapped in different paper and hidden in her closet until Friday.

"It's the video game," she realized.

"Yeah, I didn't have a chance to get the jacket."

"And you're telling me now—two days before his birthday?" She kept her voice down so that Dylan wouldn't hear, but the low volume didn't disguise her anger or frustration.

"I don't need this crap from you, Allison. Not today."

The urge to slap him was so strong that her palm actually tingled in anticipation of making contact with his cheek. Instead, she shoved her hand into her pocket. "I think the problem is that I haven't given you nearly enough crap over the past six years. Dammit, Jeff, your son shouldn't be an afterthought."

"Hey, Dad." The subject of their discussion came running into the living room, his jacket already on. "I'm ready to go."

Jeff ruffled his hair. "I'm sorry, buddy, but I'm going to have to cancel tonight."

"Oh." Dylan's face fell.

"But I brought your birthday present."

The boy perked up a little at the sight of the gift. "Can I open it now?"

"Of course," his dad said.

He dutifully opened the card first, read the message, then tore off the bow and ripped open the paper. "Oh, wow. Cool."

"Is that the one you wanted?"

Dylan's head bobbed up and down. "This is the one where you can race all the big-name tracks or make your own. Do you wanna play it with me?"

"I wish I could," Jeff said. "But I can't stay tonight. Another time, though, I promise."

The boy nodded again, but with much less enthusiasm this time.

Jeff gave him a hug. "I'll see you soon, buddy."

"Okay."

As their son retreated back to his room, Allison walked her ex-husband to the door.

"Thanks for being so understanding, Allison."

"Don't thank me," she told him. "Because I *don't* understand—and neither does that little boy in there."

"He didn't seem too disappointed," Jeff said, obviously because it eased his conscience to believe it was true.

She just shook her head and opened the door to expedite his departure.

But with her own bout of the flu a recent and vivid memory, she couldn't help but feel sorry for what Jocelyn and Jillian were going through. "I hope the girls are feeling better soon."

Her ex-husband nodded. "I'll give Dylan a call on Friday.

"I'm sure he'd appreciate that."

And she knew Dylan would be happy to talk to his dad if Jeff did call, but she also knew he wouldn't sit around waiting for the phone to ring.

She closed the door and went to find Dylan. The video game had been tossed on his desk, on top of his homework, and he was lying on his bed, music blasting from his iPod.

She reached down to pluck the earbuds from his ears. "Come on—we're going out for dinner."

"Where?" he asked cautiously.

"How about Eli's Burgers & Fries?"

He pumped his fist in the air. "Yesss!"

"Then go get your shoes on."

She didn't have to tell him twice. He raced to the mat by the door to get his sneakers. She had her own coat and shoes on when she remembered the shepherd's pie that she'd taken out of the freezer when she'd thought she'd be eating alone tonight.

She detoured to the kitchen to put the container in the fridge. Of course, Dylan followed.

"Why are we going out to eat if you had shepherd's pie?"

"I decided I wasn't in the mood for shepherd's pie."

"It's because I was supposed to go out with Dad, isn't it?"

Her son, so wise beyond his years, and still a little boy at heart. "Are you going to question my motives or open the door so we can go get burgers?"

He reached for the door.

A bacon cheeseburger with curly fries and a chocolate shake were special treats for the middle of the week, but as she tucked Dylan into bed later that night, she worried that his birthday would end up being a disappointment to him.

She didn't believe in spoiling him, and he didn't always get what he wanted, but she knew the jacket was a big deal. He hadn't been too disappointed that it wasn't under the tree at Christmas, because his birthday hadn't been too far away.

Now his birthday was in two days and she knew he wasn't going to be happy with two copies of the same video game. Which meant that she had less than forty-eight hours to get her hands on a Ren D'Alesio jacket.

Chapter Ten

In the five weeks that he'd been in the CFO's office, Nathan had never heard Allison raise her voice to anyone. In fact, in all the years that she'd worked as his uncle's executive assistant, he'd never heard her sound anything but poised and professional. But Thursday afternoon, when he came back into the office after lunch with his brother, she sounded desperate.

"I'm calling from Charisma, North Carolina," she informed whoever was on the other end of the phone she had tucked between her ear and her shoulder. "The fact that your warehouse in California *might* have stock doesn't do me any good."

She clicked through search results on her computer screen as she listened to the reply on the other end of the line.

"Yes, Kentucky is closer," she acknowledged. "But still not a viable option when I need it tomorrow."

She nodded grimly. "You're absolutely right. I shouldn't have waited until the last minute. Thank you for your help," she said, then slammed the receiver into the cradle.

"Problem?" Nate asked.

She looked up at him. "I didn't hear you come in."

"Apparently." He leaned over her desk to look at her computer screen. "What are you doing?"

"Not shopping," she grumbled. "That would require actually finding what I need in order to buy it."

"What do you need?"

"A Ren D'Alesio jacket in youth L."

He unclipped his iPhone from his belt and started to text a message. "What's the occasion?"

She rubbed her eyes with the heels of her hands and sighed. "Dylan's birthday."

"When?"

"Tomorrow."

His brows rose. "The way you run things around here, I would have guessed you were the kind of mom who would have her son's presents all wrapped and ready two weeks before his birthday."

"*I* was giving him the video game he wanted—which *is* wrapped and ready," she said in her defense. "His dad said he would get the jacket, and then he showed up last night and gave Dylan the game."

His gaze shifted to the screen to read his brother's reply. "Miscommunication?"

Tears of frustration shone in her eyes. "Something like that."

But he could tell by the tension in her voice that it was a lot more than that.

"If your son's a Ren D'Alesio fan, I assume you know that he drives the number seven-twenty-two car for Garrett/Slater Racing and that my brother Daniel is part owner of that team?"

"I do," she agreed.

"So why didn't you ask me if I might be able to help with your birthday present dilemma?"

"I want to say that it was because I wouldn't feel right exploiting our working relationship for personal reasons, but the truth is, I was going to exhaust all other options first."

"Have you exhausted all those other options?"

She sighed. "Pretty much."

"And if I told you that Daniel is going to ensure that a youth L jacket is delivered here by noon tomorrow?" He held up his phone, showing her the confirmation he'd just received from his brother.

Her jaw actually dropped open. "For real?"

He nodded.

"I wouldn't know how I could possibly repay you," she said sincerely.

"You could say 'thank you' and invite me to come over for a piece of birthday cake," he suggested.

"Birthday cake?"

"It's a cake, usually decorated in honor of the occasion, sometimes with an appropriate number of candles to indicate the year being celebrated."

"I know what it is—I'm just not sure I understand why you want a piece of my son's birthday cake."

"I like cake," he said simply.

She closed the tabs linking her to several different online retailers. "Do you like spaghetti, too?"

"As a matter of fact, I do."

"Then you can come for dinner before the cake," she offered. "If you want."

"I'd like that."

"We usually eat at six."

"I'll be there," he told her.

"I should warn you—we don't often have guests for dinner, and Dylan can be extremely shy around people he doesn't know."

"I promise that I won't ask him to entertain me with a stand-up comedy routine—at least, not before cake."

Her lips curved, just a little. "Good call."

As Nate made his way to his own desk, he realized he was already looking forward to the following night.

Her son wasn't a fan of parties.

Allison had learned that when Dylan was in kindergarten and she'd invited five kids from his class to celebrate his fifth birthday. She'd invited Jeff and Jodie and the girls, too, but Jillian was just an infant and Jodie had been terrified of exposing her to the germs of so many other children, so they'd declined.

Notwithstanding their absence, Allison thought the party was a big hit—with everyone except the birthday boy. His guests had happily run around the apartment and played party games, eaten pizza and ice cream cake. But Dylan—a typical only child and atypical child—didn't like chaos and he didn't like anyone else touching his stuff.

Since then, she'd kept their celebrations simple and the guest list small. In fact, Allison and Dylan usually celebrated the occasion alone, unless "Aunt Chelsea" was available to join them. But Chelsea was working tonight, and Dylan was pouting despite the fact that she'd dropped off a gift on her way to the bar. The revelation that Mr. Garrett would be coming for dinner did not appease him.

He did seem pleased with the decorations, though. The Happy Birthday banner Allison had pinned to the dining room wall was flanked by bouquets of balloons, and the cake—chocolate with cherry filling and chocolate whipped icing from The Sweet Spot—was on the sideboard with nine candles strategically placed around his name. The jacket, delivered to the office earlier that day as promised, was wrapped in festive paper topped with a big red bow.

"When are we gonna eat?" Dylan wanted to know.

"About fifteen minutes after Mr. Garrett gets here," she explained for the tenth time. She didn't want to overcook the pasta, so she was waiting for Nate to arrive before she dumped it into the boiling water.

"Why is your boss coming to my birthday party?"

It didn't matter to Dylan that there would be only three of them at the table—the fact that it was his birthday and there were balloons and cake was enough to make it a party.

Because he's the only reason that you're getting what

you most want for your birthday. Of course, aloud she said only, "Because I thought it would be nice to invite him to have dinner with us."

Dylan plucked at a loose thread on the hem of his sweater. "Is he…your boyfriend?"

"What? *No.*"

"Oh." Her son sounded almost disappointed. "Why don't you have a boyfriend?"

Allison stirred the sauce that was simmering on the stove and wondered if she would ever understand the way her son's mind worked. "I don't have time for a boyfriend."

"Why not?"

"Because I'm too busy doing my job and being a mom and answering all of your questions."

He smiled at that. "But what about when I'm not here? Why don't you have a boyfriend then?"

"Because that's when I clean the house and do the laundry."

"Miss Aberdeen has a job *and* a boyfriend," he told her, naming his third grade teacher. "And they're gonna get married in the summer."

"That's great for her." And it explained the origin of his questions.

"Are you ever gonna to get married again?"

"I don't know, Dylan. But it's not a priority right now."

"I think you should get married again."

"Why is that?"

"Because I'm prob'ly not gonna live at home forever. One of these days, when I get a wife, I'm gonna have to find a place of my own."

"That's true," she agreed, holding back her smile.

"And when I move out, I don't want you to be lonely."

She slung an arm across his shoulders and pulled him close so that she could kiss the top of his head. "I appreciate your concern," she told him sincerely. "But I think we've got a few years before we need to worry about that."

He shrugged. "I dunno. Kayleigh Tippett said that she's gonna marry me."

Kayleigh Tippett lived in the apartment building across the street and was in Dylan's class at school. "And how do you feel about that?"

"I dunno," he said again. "She always shares her cookies with me, but she's kinda bossy."

"Then it's probably best if you keep your options open," she suggested, and breathed a sigh of relief when the intercom buzzed.

Of course, Nate's arrival meant the abrupt departure of her curious chatterbox son and the appearance of his extremely shy and introverted alter ego. But considering Dylan's chosen topic of conversation, she decided that wasn't a bad thing.

Dylan Caldwell was the shyest, quietest and most polite child Nate had ever met.

Not that he'd met a lot of kids, but it was inevitable that they crossed his path on occasion. And usually when they did, they were moving at full speed and full volume.

Andrew's daughter, Maura, was almost the same age as Allison's son, but that was about the only thing the two children had in common. His adorable niece didn't seem to understand the meaning of the words *quiet* or *still*. Dylan, by contrast, sat unobtrusively at the table, only answering questions that were directed to him, and even then, he did so with as few words as possible.

When Allison invited him to dinner, he thought it would be a good chance to spend some time with her son. Knowing how she doted on the boy, he figured that establishing a good rapport with him would be a step closer to Allison. Unfortunately, the kid didn't say more than a dozen words to him throughout the meal. He didn't say much more than that to his mother, but they seemed to have their own form of shorthand communication, no doubt a result of the fact that it had been just the two of them for so long. He felt as though he was on the outside looking in—and it surprised him to realize that he wished he was on the inside with them.

On a more positive note, the food was delicious. In addition to the spaghetti that Allison had promised, there was a green salad and crispy garlic bread.

When dinner was finished and the dishes cleared away, Allison lit the candles on the cake and set it in front of her son. Dylan raised himself up on his knees on the seat of the chair and closed his eyes tight as he made his wish and blew hard to extinguish each one of the nine candles.

Dylan opened his gift from Aunt Chelsea first—a Ren D'Alesio baseball cap and a book about the history of stock car racing. Allison handed him Nate's gift next—a limited edition die-cast scale replica model of the number 722 car. Dylan looked at him, his dark eyes—so much like his mother's—wide with awe.

"Your mom mentioned that you were a fan," Nate said.

The boy nodded. "I've never seen one like this," he admitted. "It's awesome. Thanks."

When Allison set her own gift on the table in front of him, Dylan bit down on his lower lip. He'd probably guessed, based on the size of the box, what was inside, and his excitement was palpable. At the same time, he almost seemed afraid to open it—just in case it wasn't what he wanted. No wonder Allison had been so eager to get the jacket for her son, and it made Nate grateful that he'd been able to help.

When Dylan was finally given the cue to open his last gift, he tore away the paper and ripped apart the box—and the look on his face when he lifted the jacket out of the box was one of stunned amazement.

"This is…" He seemed to be at a loss for words as he ran

his hands over the various crests, reverently traced the outline of the driver's number, then the replicated signature. In the end, he simply finished with, "Wow."

Then he slid off of his chair to wrap his arms around his mother and hug her tight. "Thank you! Thank you! Thank you!"

Allison smiled as she returned the embrace. As her eyes met Nate's over her son's head, she mouthed, *Thank you.*

He just nodded and hoped she'd still be grateful when Dylan found what was tucked inside the pocket of the jacket.

"Are you just going to look at it or are you going to try it on?" she asked.

Dylan grinned and slipped his arms into the sleeves. It was a little big, but she no doubt wanted to make sure he'd be able to wear it for more than one season.

He snapped the buttons to close the front, then tucked his hands in his pockets. His brow furrowed. "There's something in here."

"Probably tags," Allison guessed.

He pulled his hand out. "It's an envelope," he realized, and opened the flap. "And there's tickets inside."

"Tickets?" Allison looked from her son to Nate.

Of course, his deliberately neutral expression gave nothing away. But as Dylan's smile spread, she started to feel uneasy.

"For the race in Bristol."

Race? As in stock car race? Judging by the pure, unadulterated joy on her son's face, she'd guess her assumption was correct. And she hated that she would have to crush his enthusiasm.

"I don't know how those tickets got in there," she said, though her narrowed gaze shifted to Nate, suggesting otherwise. "But—"

"Don't say we can't go," Dylan interrupted. "Please, Mom. It's *Bristol*."

"Is that supposed to mean something to me?"

"It's the world's fastest half mile," her son explained.

"And Bristol is in Tennessee." She might not know stock car racing, but she knew geography. "And Tennessee is about a four-hour drive from here."

"Or an hour flight," Nate interjected.

"Not helping," she said.

Dylan looked at Nate, his excitement over the possibility overcoming his innate shyness—at least for the moment. "We could fly?"

"No, we cannot fly," Allison told him—both of them.

Her son looked at her pleadingly. "But I've never been on a plane."

"Because we can't afford—"

"Flights and accommodations are included with the tickets," Nate spoke up again.

Allison drew in a slow, deep breath and reminded herself that she had to handle this carefully or her son would never forgive her. But she was furious with Nate, that he'd gone ahead and made arrangements without even talking to her. And she was frustrated that he could give her son an opportunity that she never could. "Which is incredibly generous, but not something I could ever repay."

"It's a gift," Nate reminded her. "No repayment required."

"The model car was a gift. This is—"

"The best gift ever!" Dylan announced.

And in his eyes, it undoubtedly was, but even her son's enthusiasm couldn't override her reservations. Or silence the questions that echoed in her mind: Why was Nate doing this? What did he hope to gain?

"Why don't you go into the living room to play your new video game while Mr. Garrett helps me clear the table?" she suggested to Dylan.

Her son—thrilled to be released from his usual after-dinner chores in addition to his gifts—didn't need to be told twice.

"You're mad," Nathan guessed.

"You're perceptive." She stacked the cake plates and carried them to the kitchen to load into the dishwasher.

"Do you want me to apologize?"

She glanced up at him. "Are you sorry?"

"No," he admitted, setting the glasses on the counter.

"But you'd apologize anyway?"

"If it would stop you being mad at me."

She wiped her hands on a towel. "I'm not just mad, I'm infuriated. And I know I should be grateful—you've given him an opportunity that I never could. But I don't feel comfortable with the whole setup and I'm not sure why you'd go to so much trouble when—"

"I meant what I said," he interrupted to reassure her. "It's a gift. No payment required and no strings attached."

His generosity wasn't just overwhelming, it was baffling. "Why?"

"Because the way you described the whole family situation, it seemed to me like the kid's got a pretty rotten deal in the past and I figured it was time he got to do something that was all about him. I also thought that you might enjoy doing it with him so that, years from now, when he thinks back to his first stock car race, you'll be part of that memory."

She sighed, because he was absolutely right—she just hadn't expected him to be able to read the situation so accurately. "And, as you can see, he's thrilled by the prospect of going to Bristol."

"But you're wondering if this is all some kind of elaborate ploy to get you back into my bed," he guessed.

"It crossed my mind," she admitted. "But I can't imagine you'd go to that much effort for any woman."

"I would—for you," he said.

The admission unnerved her as much as the sincerity in his tone.

"Make no mistake, Alli—I do want you back in my bed. But when we make love again, it's going to be because you want me, too, not because you're feeling obligated or grateful."

Her traitorous heart hammered against her ribs. "Don't you mean *if*?"

"No, I mean *when*," he confirmed. "But the timetable is entirely in your hands."

"I thought…I mean…you never gave any indication… that you still wanted me."

"I haven't stopped wanting you," he assured her. "But I also wanted to make sure you knew that anything that happens between us outside of the office has nothing to do with work."

She nodded. "Are *you* going to Bristol?"

"Of course—the kid needs someone with him who knows what's going on."

She smiled at that. "But we wouldn't be sharing a room in Tennessee?"

"I don't have a lot of experience with kids, but even I'm smart enough to know that probably wouldn't be an arrangement that would work for you." He waited a beat. "Would it?"

She couldn't help but smile at the hopeful tone in his voice. "No, it wouldn't."

He sighed. "Then it's a good thing I've already booked separate rooms."

She was making coffee for Nate when Dylan ventured into the kitchen. He hovered in the background for a minute, as if trying to summon up the courage to say something. Conversation with new people had never come easily to him, and he'd already interacted with Nathan more than she'd anticipated.

"Do you want to play my new race game, Mr…Nate?" he

finally asked, remembering that Nate had insisted he call him by his given name.

Initiating conversation was a huge step for Dylan, and she could tell by the tone of his voice that he didn't hold out much hope of his invitation being accepted. She held her breath to see how Nate would respond, not just to the question but to her son.

"Can I be the number seven-twenty-two car?" he asked.

Dylan shook his head without even considering the request. "Nuh-uh—only I get to drive that one."

Nate sighed. "Four-fourteen?"

"Sure," her son agreed. "But we're racing Pocono so be careful on turn three—you don't want your back end to step out."

"I'll be careful on turn three," Nate promised.

He started to follow Dylan out of the room, then realized that he was abandoning Allison to finish the cleanup on her own. "Do you mind?" he asked her.

She shook her head. "No, I don't mind."

But as they went off to play video games together, she found herself questioning the truthfulness of her response. She couldn't object to her boss paying attention to her son, but in light of Dylan's recent interest in finding her a boyfriend, she was a little wary.

Because it was Friday night, and because it was his birthday, she let Dylan stay up past his usual bedtime. But at nine o'clock, she insisted that the current race was the last one. As they zoomed toward the finish line, each one trying to nudge the other out of the way, Allison was sure they were both going to crash and let the orange car running in third win the checkered flag. But Dylan assured her they were only "trading paint" and then, when he edged out Nate's car at the finish, he had to spin in circles, tearing up the infield before making his way to victory lane.

When the celebrations were finally done and Winner finished flashing on the screen, she directed her son to the shower. He didn't grumble too much, and he high-fived Nate on the way out and thanked him again for the "awesome" birthday present before going to do his mother's bidding.

"You want to see if you can beat me, too?" Nate asked, gesturing with his controller.

She shook her head. "I can't even watch Dylan play for too long without feeling dizzy."

Nate put both controllers back in the basket beneath the table, then reached for Allison's hand. He linked their fingers together and tugged her down onto the cushion beside him.

Sitting close to Nate made her feel dizzy, too, but in a completely different way. She wondered if she should shift to the other end of the sofa, to put some distance between them. But sitting close beside him, the warm strength of his thigh against hers, felt good. Maybe too good.

Over the past several weeks, she'd ignored her feelings for Nate, convinced that he was no longer interested and, even if he was, that he couldn't ever fit into her life. It was a well-known fact that he didn't do relationships, that he had no interest in a family of his own. But it had taken only five minutes of watching him with her son to have her questioning what she thought she knew about him.

And Dylan had basked in the undivided attention. She knew that her son loved his father and enjoyed his time with Jeff, but recently, there had been little time or attention that was his exclusively. She didn't blame Jeff for that—or she tried not to. She understood that he had a new wife and other children who needed him, too. But they were a cohesive family unit, and she wanted more for Dylan than stolen moments of time shared with siblings who had the benefit of living with both of their parents.

Nathan had given more time and attention to Dylan in three hours tonight than Jeff had done in the past three weeks. She knew it wasn't a fair comparison. Her boss had no personal obligations, no demands on his time. And seeing how quickly her son had overcome his usual reticence with him—no doubt helped along by the excited anticipation of seeing a live stock car race—only added to her concerns about the weekend they were going to spend together in Bristol.

Yes, she was worried about Dylan's expectations, but she was even more worried about her own.

Chapter Eleven

"What are you thinking about that put that furrow back between your brows?" Nate asked.

Allison shook her head. "Nothing, really."

"I don't think you have any reason to worry about Dylan—he's a great kid, Alli."

She smiled at that. "I think so."

"It's obvious that you have a good relationship with him."

"I try," she said. "Unfortunately, every day isn't cake and ice cream."

She heard the water shut off in the bathroom and shifted to the end of the sofa, away from Nate.

His brows lifted.

"I don't want Dylan getting the wrong idea about us."

"We were having a conversation—not making out."

"He already asked if you were my boyfriend."

"Why would he ask that?"

"Because I'm not in the habit of inviting men over for dinner."

"So what did you tell him?"

"The truth."

"You told him that we're not dating but we sometimes have earth-shattering sex together?"

Her cheeks flushed. "Just the first part because the 'have' is now a 'had' and therefore irrelevant."

"So you don't think about me anymore?"

"I think—no, I *know*—that a personal relationship with my boss is a recipe for disaster."

"You're the only one who gives a damn about my title."

"You don't think people in the office would have something to say if we started dating? You don't think your family would have something to say?"

"I don't care what other people think—even the people related to me. And you're more naive than I would have guessed if you honestly believe no one at the office suspects we've been seeing each other."

"Well, I do care," she said. "And *suspecting* isn't the same thing as *knowing*." But she couldn't deny that even the possibility of speculation bothered her.

"Why is this such a big issue for you?" he asked.

"There were two reasons I was thrilled to be hired at Garrett Furniture," she told him.

"The former CFO's handsome nephew being one of those reasons?"

She chuckled. "The former CFO has a lot of handsome nephews—and you were still in New York when I started working for your uncle."

"So what were the reasons?" he prompted.

"On-site day care and medical benefits. And while Dylan has obviously outgrown the need for day care, he has asthma, so the medical benefits are still essential."

"How bad is his asthma?"

"Not bad at all, on a day-to-day basis. But every once in a while, it's terrifying."

"I can't imagine," he admitted.

"He had a rough go of it when he was younger. He was in and out of the hospital a lot before he was properly diagnosed and we were able to get it under control."

"Well, you don't need to worry about medical benefits. Your job is not in jeopardy," he assured her. "No matter what happens between us, I promise you that."

"How can you make that promise?"

"I'm the boss," he reminded her. "And your employment is specifically protected by paragraph 114.6 of the Employee Handbook."

"I'll check that out," she said. "But right now, I should check on Dylan—make sure he's brushed his teeth and is tucked into bed."

"Is that my cue to leave?"

She shrugged. "It's getting late."

It wasn't really, but now that Dylan had left the room, they were both aware of the attraction sizzling in the air. An attraction that she hadn't decided what to do about and that he wasn't willing to act on with her son so close by.

He stood up and she followed him to the door, then offered her hand.

He took it, choosing to be amused rather than insulted by the gesture, and held it for a long moment, letting his thumb brush lightly over her knuckles, watching the awareness darken her eyes.

"Thanks for dinner."

"Thank *you*," she said. "Not just for the jacket but everything. You made Dylan's birthday celebration something truly special."

"Does that mean you're over being mad about the tickets?"

"It means that I'm getting there. Slowly."

"So I probably shouldn't do anything else to set you off."

"You shouldn't do anything else to set me off," she agreed.

"Would a good-night kiss be considered 'anything else'?"

"It might fit into that category."

"Then I guess—" his lips feathered lightly over hers "—I shouldn't—" and again "—kiss you good-night."

She closed her eyes, for just a second, as if savoring the

fleeting contact, then pressed her lips together. "You definitely…shouldn't…kiss me."

"Then I'll just say good night, Alli."

"Good night, Nate."

Chelsea stopped by to have coffee with Allison Saturday morning, which was clearly just an excuse to pry for details about dinner the night before.

"So how was your birthday, Dilly Bug?" she asked, when the sleepy-eyed boy finally wandered into the kitchen.

"Awesome!"

"Did you get cool stuff?"

"Really cool," he confirmed. And although Allison knew he was most excited about the upcoming trip to Bristol, he remembered to thank his "aunt" for her gift. "I'm gonna wear it for sure when we go to the race."

Chelsea sent Allison a questioning look before she focused her attention back on Dylan. "What race?"

"We're going to the fastest half-mile in the world."

"Bristol?" Chelsea immediately guessed, because working part-time in a sports bar for a dozen years had taught her almost everything anyone needed to know about sports—and more.

The little boy nodded enthusiastically. "Mom got me a D'Alesio jacket and there were tickets in the pocket."

"That's a lucky bonus."

"And Nate said we're gonna go on an airplane so we can be there to watch qualifying and everything." He opened the pantry and pulled out a box of his favorite cereal.

"Nate?" she said, looking at Allison, who busied herself pulling the milk out of the fridge for Dylan.

"Nate Garrett—Mom's boss." He dumped the cereal into a bowl, poured some milk over it, then took a spoon from the drawer.

"Sounds like a fun trip."

He nodded again, then looked at his mom. "Can I take this in the living room? I wanna watch qualifying."

"Go ahead," Allison agreed, albeit reluctantly. Because she knew that as soon as her son left the room, she would be inundated with questions.

Sure enough, Chelsea waited only until she heard the television come on in the other room before she asked, "Is it true? Are you really going to Tennessee with Nate Garrett?"

She nodded. "Tell me I'm not crazy."

"You're crazy," Chelsea said.

"Not quite the reassurance I was hoping for."

"You're the one who said that you couldn't risk any kind of personal involvement with your boss. And you don't even like stock car racing."

"I know. But Dylan does—and Nate set up this whole weekend for him, so how could I say no?"

"How you've managed to say no to anything the man asks is beyond me," Chelsea admitted. "And now, he did this—without any prompting—for your son?"

"I only asked if he could get the jacket. Actually, I didn't even get around to asking him that much—he knew I was having trouble finding it, so he asked his brother to help."

"Gotta love a man who takes charge," Chelsea said approvingly.

"My ex-husband liked to take charge," Allison reminded her.

"No, he liked to tell you what to do," her friend countered. "And he still does."

Allison couldn't deny it.

"In all the years that I've known Nate, I've never heard of him taking chicken soup to a sick friend or making plans to spend a weekend with a woman and her kid. And now he's taking you and your nine-year-old son to Bristol, making Dylan's biggest wish come true… Are you sharing a room?"

"No! Of course not."

"So he's done all of that and not even getting sex in return? That man is seriously smitten."

"Maybe he's hoping to get lucky despite insisting he has no expectations."

"He's a guy—of course he's hoping," Chelsea said. "But the fact that he's letting the choice be yours speaks volumes. He doesn't just want sex—he wants *you*." She got up to pour more coffee into her mug. "So—are you going to sleep with him?"

"No."

Her friend rolled her eyes. "He's one of the hottest single guys in Charisma—you could at least take a minute to think it over."

"I've spent a lot of minutes thinking about it," Allison confided, because Chelsea was her best friend and the only person she could admit it to. "But I can't do it—sleeping with the boss would make me a horrible cliché."

"Not if the sex was good," Chelsea countered. "Then it would make you a smart woman—and a satisfied employee."

She sighed, a little wistfully. "The sex would be great."

"So maybe you need to rethink your plans," her friend suggested.

"I can't," Allison insisted. "Because I know that one night would only make me want more."

"Why can't you have more?" Chelsea asked.

"Because Nate doesn't do more."

"It's March—almost two months since the night you spent together in St. Louis, which means that this is probably the longest relationship he's ever had with a woman."

"Except for the fact that we don't have a relationship."

"I think you do," Chelsea insisted. "You just don't want to admit it because you're as wary about relationships as he is."

"I'm not wary," she denied. "I'm just focusing on my son—that's the most important relationship in my life."

"So what does my Dilly Bug think of your new boyfriend?"

"He's not my boyfriend."

Chelsea just laughed.

She was starting to pack for the trip when Dylan was out with his dad Wednesday night. After saying goodbye to his son, Jeff asked to speak with her for a minute.

"Is something wrong?"

"No, I just wanted you to know that Jodie cleared our schedule for Saturday afternoon so we can take Dylan to Buster's to make up for missing his birthday."

She wondered if he would ever ask rather than tell her his plans. Of course, she knew it was at least partially her own fault that she'd always let him dictate the schedule of his visitation with Dylan because she wanted her son to spend as much time as possible with his father. But this time, she shook her head. "Sorry, that won't work."

"Why not?"

"Because we already have plans for the weekend."

"Change them," Jeff suggested.

"I can't."

He frowned. "Come on, Allison. I know I was short with you that night and I'm sorry, but it's not like you to hold a grudge."

"I'm not holding a grudge," she assured him. "And if we weren't going away, Dylan would be happy to go with you."

His scowl deepened. "Where are you going?"

"Tennessee."

"Why on earth would you go to Tennessee?"

"For the race at Bristol this weekend."

"You don't know the first thing about stock car racing."

She shrugged. "Apparently I'm going to learn."

"How did you manage to get tickets?"

"Garrett Furniture is one of the sponsors of the number seven-twenty-two car," she reminded him.

"And so they're giving out tickets to the employee of the month?"

"I mentioned to my boss that Dylan was a huge race fan, so Nate got the tickets for him for his birthday."

She'd never been a good liar, and though it wasn't really a lie, it wasn't the whole truth, and her ex-husband picked up on that. "Jesus, Allison—tell me you're not screwing him."

She was shocked by the crude choice of words as much as the question, and though it was none of his business if she was "screwing" Nate Garrett or anyone else, she had to ask, "Where did that come from?"

"Dylan told me that your boyfriend was here for dinner on his birthday."

"Well, Dylan was mistaken."

"Nathan Garrett wasn't here?"

"He was here, but he's not my boyfriend."

"You invited your boss for dinner?"

"Not that it's any of your business who I invite over for dinner, but Nate used his connections to get the Ren D'Alesio jacket that *you* were supposed to get for Dylan for his birthday—and to thank him, I invited him to come over so that he could see Dylan open it. And Nate gave us the tickets."

"Is he going to Tennessee with you?"

"He's going to Bristol for the race," she confirmed.

"I don't approve of this, Allison."

"Well, then, it's a good thing I don't need or want your approval."

"You need that job," he reminded her. "I don't have the kind of medical benefits that you do and all those inhalers Dylan needs cost a fortune."

"I'm well aware of our son's medical needs," she said coolly.

"Then don't jeopardize your job because you've got a crush on your boss."

She opened the door to hasten his exit. "Thanks for the advice—I'll see you next week."

The kid was practically vibrating with nervous energy.

Dylan was buckled into his seat beside his mother, his gaze glued to the sky outside the window, but he kept wrapping the loose end of the belt around his hand, then unwrapping it again.

Nate was a little apprehensive, too, because there was a lot riding on this weekend. He'd never had any concerns about hanging out with Andrew's daughter, Maura, but he'd never worried about making a good impression on her, either. Maybe the fact that she was his niece took some of the pressure off, because even if he said or did something stupid, their relationship was solid. But he barely knew Dylan, and he knew that if he screwed up, it would be over with Allison before it had even begun.

When Daniel had offered the tickets, he'd leaped at the chance to take Allison and her son to the race. It had seemed the perfect opportunity to win the kid over—or at least make a favorable first impression. But now he was wondering if he'd gone too big too soon. Maybe he should have started with a ninety-minute weekend matinee instead of a three-day weekend out of town.

He'd never fallen in love with stock car racing the way his younger brother had, but since Daniel had gone into partnership with Josh Slater and founded GSR, he'd come to appreciate the energy and excitement that surrounded every aspect of the sport. He thought it would be fun to share that with Allison's son. The boy was, in Nate's opinion, far too serious and quiet—except when Dylan talked about racing. Then his eyes lit up and enthusiasm filled his voice so that he looked and sounded like almost any other nine-year-old kid Nate had ever met.

Now that they were in the air and on their way to Bristol, Nate was thinking he should have opted for a race closer to home. Somewhere like Charlotte or Martinsville, where they could have gone to the race and returned home the same day. That way, if the experience was a complete bust, it would be over relatively quickly. Instead, he'd decided that a whole weekend was a good idea. He'd rarely ever spent a whole weekend with a woman, never mind a woman and her kid.

And Dylan looked as wary as Nate felt. Maybe it was the flight—Allison had told him that her son had never been on an airplane before.

"So what do you think of flying?" Nate asked him.

"I didn't think the plane would be so small," Dylan said.

"None of the major airlines fly direct from Raleigh to Bristol," he said, explaining why he'd decided to charter a plane for the trip. "And this is a six-seat Piper, owned by my friend Anthony—who also happens to be the pilot. If you have any questions about how the plane stays in the air, I'm sure he'd be happy to answer them."

The kid shook his head. "I looked it up. I know all about lift, gravity, thrust and drag."

"Then maybe you could answer his questions," he said.

Dylan frowned at that, as if he didn't get that Nate was joking. Allison covered her son's hand with her own, squeezed it.

Nate tried again. "Are you interested in aerodynamics?"

The kid shrugged. "I just like to know about a lot of things."

"There's nothing wrong with that," he assured him. "We wouldn't be able to fly to Bristol today if the Wright brothers hadn't displayed the same kind of curiosity."

"But sometimes I ask too many questions."

"I've noticed that you're quite the gabber."

It took the boy a minute, but this time he realized that Nate was only teasing, and he offered a shy smile in response.

"Mom's gonna have lots of questions this weekend," Dylan warned. "She doesn't know anything about racing."

"I know about restrictor plates now," she said.

"They don't use restrictor plates at Bristol," her son told her.

"Why not?"

"Because it's a short track."

"Oh."

But it was clear from her tone that she still didn't make the connection. Nate winked at Dylan, and the kid offered another shy smile in return.

"So if the race is on Sunday, why are we going to the track today?" Allison asked.

"Because before the drivers can race for the checkered flag, they have to qualify."

She frowned at that. "You mean, we might have come all this way and not even get to see Ren D'Alesio race?"

"He'll qualify," Dylan said with unwavering confidence.

"How does he qualify?"

As Anthony brought the plane smoothly down, Dylan patiently explained the procedure to his mother—the first-round qualifying that would take place on Friday, and the advantages of making that first cut, then the second round Saturday morning, and why some drivers would choose to stand on their time from the first round rather than participate in the second round.

The boy had obviously watched a lot of races and paid attention to the commentators. But if he'd never actually been to a race, he couldn't know how it really felt to be part of the action. The vibration of the ground beneath his feet as forty-plus cars rushed past so fast their distinctive paint schemes were nothing more than a blur of color.

The speedway was about a twenty-minute drive from the airport, and on the way, Dylan filled his mom in on Ren D'Alesio's stats—number of races, poles, wins and top-ten finishes. But he fell silent again when they arrived at the track and merged with the crowd of people.

The kid gaped at the lineup of haulers, their exteriors showcasing the colors, numbers and sponsors of the respective teams. He looked eagerly for the 722 hauler and seemed to be as much in awe of it as Nate suspected he would be when he got to see the actual vehicle Ren would be driving.

When they finally spotted the distinctive gold-and-green car, it was being checked over by the race inspectors, easily identified by OFFICIAL spelled out in block letters on their backs.

"What do the officials do?" Allison asked.

Nate waited to see if Dylan would answer, but the boy was too busy watching the inspection to pay any attention to his mother's question.

"They inspect the cars before every race to ensure that they're in compliance with the regulations of the specific track."

"What happens if a vehicle isn't in compliance?"

"It has to be fixed before the car can be put on the track for qualifying."

Dylan moved away from the fence as the 722 car was waved through.

"I didn't realize it was so technical," she admitted.

"She thought it was just a bunch of guys in fast cars who didn't know how to turn right," Dylan told him.

He looked at Allison, his brows raised.

Her cheeks colored. "That's what it looks like on TV," she said, just a little defensively.

"You've got a lot to learn," Nate said, as Dylan nodded his agreement.

They tracked down Daniel when they followed the 722

car back to the garage. He shook his brother's hand, said hello to Allison and put a lanyard around Dylan's neck.

The kid looked down at the hot pass inside the plastic cover, then back at Daniel with wordless awe, as if he'd just been handed the keys to the kingdom. And to a nine-year-old race fan, a hot pass was exactly that.

"What is it?" Allison asked, as Daniel gave matching lanyards to both her and Nate.

Dylan, who could probably give her an official definition and recite all the perks, was silent, stunned.

"It gives you access the garage and pit road, even when the track goes hot."

"Goes hot?" she echoed uncertainly.

"Usually an hour before the start of the race, everyone without a hot pass has to clear out of the area," Daniel clarified for her. "But today, with that pass, you can watch qualifying from up on top of the pit box if you want."

Dylan found his voice. "For real?"

Daniel chuckled. "For real. But you'll have to hang around awhile, because Ren is in the second half for qualifying."

Nate bought them pizza slices and soft drinks before they went to the watch the qualifying.

The crew chief was already on top of the pit box when they arrived, and he had headphones for all of them—to combat the noise, he explained, and so they could listen in to the communications between the driver and the garage.

Dylan followed the instructions he was given without question. He sat where he was told to sit, he put the headphones on and he settled back to watch. Only about a dozen cars had done their laps when Nate noticed that Allison was watching her son rather than the track. He shifted closer, so that he could talk to her without everyone on top of the pit box hearing their conversation. "Is something wrong?"

"I didn't realize the smells would be so strong."

"Race fuel and hot rubber," Nate told her.

"I'm fine, Mom," Dylan interjected, obviously more aware of the reason for her concern.

"His asthma," she said to Nate.

"Oh. Right." She'd mentioned it to him once before, but he wasn't entirely sure he understood what it meant. "We can move to the grandstand, if it's a problem."

"It's not a problem," Dylan said. Then, to his mom, "I've got my inhaler."

She hesitated a moment, then nodded.

But while Dylan watched the cars circle the track, she spent more time watching him.

When the first round of qualifying was complete—with Ren making the cut that exempted him from having to re-qualify the next day—they headed back to the hauler. Ren and Mike, his crew chief, were hanging out there, already looking forward to the race and discussing minor adjustments that should be made to the car before then. Ren felt the car had more to give and believed that if he'd pushed a little harder, he might have gotten the pole. His fastest lap had been less than half a second slower than the leader, but still only good enough for thirteenth spot.

Allison didn't seem to be paying much attention to the content of the conversation—she seemed more caught up in the fact that her son was right in the middle of it. Nate was surprised to find that the boy's shyness had disappeared in the face of his excitement and enthusiasm, and he was glad that the weekend was proving to be everything the kid hoped and imagined.

But he still wanted more: he wanted Allison back in his bed.

Chapter Twelve

Allison couldn't remember the last time she'd seen her son so animated, and she knew that she'd never be able to repay Nate for the gift of this weekend. But she hoped that buying dinner might be a start. He agreed on the condition that Dylan got to choose where they would eat.

That was how they ended up at the '50s-style diner across the street from their hotel. The floor was tiled in black and white, with chrome stools lined up at the soda fountain and red vinyl chairs around Formica tables for other diners. The walls were decorated with framed prints of vintage cars and posters advertising classic movies. And, of course, there was a Wurlitzer jukebox in the back corner where you could choose three golden oldies for a quarter.

The menu was updated with offerings that included not just hamburgers and hot dogs but also chicken and veggie burgers, with countless variations of each, and hand-dipped milkshakes. Dylan gorged himself like any nine-year-old boy, tackling a bacon cheeseburger, curly fries and a chocolate shake. But even before he was halfway through his meal, Allison could tell that the excitement of the day was beginning to catch up with him.

After dinner, they went back to the hotel—a Sweet Dream Inn, chosen because the hotel chain was a GSR sponsor. Allison and Dylan were in suite 810, and Nate was in 812, an adjoining suite.

Dylan had a quick shower, then she tucked him into bed,

not the least bit surprised that he was asleep almost before his head hit the pillow. She puttered around the room for a little while, partly because she wanted to make sure he was completely and deeply asleep and partly because she was debating her next move.

When we make love again, it's going to be because you want me, too.

There had never been any question that she wanted Nate—the question had been more about what would come after. If she got involved with him, would he end up breaking her heart? Because she knew it would end—with Nate, there was no chance of anything else. But even knowing that, she couldn't resist what he was offering, what she wanted.

She knocked on the adjoining door.

Nate responded immediately, almost as if he'd been waiting. "Is something wrong?"

"No, everything's fine," she hastened to assure him. "Great even. I just, um, wanted to thank you. For today. For everything."

"I'm glad Dylan had a good time."

"The best," she said. "And those were his words, not mine. You've done so much for him. Not just the race, but the whole weekend."

"I was a baseball fan when I was his age," Nate confided. "And I'll never forget the thrill of meeting Cal Ripken Junior."

"He'll never forget this weekend—or the part you played in making it happen. In his eyes, you're as much a hero as Ren D'Alesio now."

"I'm not anyone's hero," he warned her.

"You were my son's today," she said. "So thank you."

"I don't want you to be grateful."

"Well, I am. You did something amazing for my son and I can't help but feel appreciative." She drew a deep breath and shored up her courage. "But that's not why I knocked on this door."

"Why did you?"

She held his gaze. "Because I thought you might be able to make one of my wishes come true, too."

"Am I correct in assuming you don't want Ren D'Alesio's autograph?"

"I don't want Ren D'Alesio's autograph," she confirmed.

Nate didn't move. "So what do you want?"

"You."

He finally stepped away from the door, and she crossed the threshold.

Nate started to push the door shut, then reconsidered. "Should we keep this open?"

Allison shook her head.

"What if Dylan wakes up—or has an asthma attack?"

"He doesn't usually wake up in the night," she told him. "But we can keep the door slightly ajar, so I'll hear him if he does."

So he closed the door, but only partially, and pulled her into his arms.

He wanted to take his time, but they'd both wanted this—and fought against it—for too long to go slow now. He had her undressed before they made it across the room to his bed. He laid her down on top of the mattress and lowered himself over her.

He sucked her breasts, pulling first one nipple into his mouth, then the other. She gasped and sighed and rocked her hips. The way she was rubbing against him, there was no denying that she was wet and ready for him.

This time he had planned ahead—just in case—and he wasted no time in tearing open a condom package and sheathing himself. Then he drove into the moist heat between her thighs.

She gasped again, and her muscles clamped around him, pulsing her pleasure. She arched beneath him, pulling him deeper, and he felt the already tenuous thread of control start to slip from his fingers.

He caught her hands, held them over her head, and pressed his body against hers, pinning her to the mattress. "This isn't a race," he admonished softly.

"But I want—"

He nibbled on her lip, halting the flow of her words. "I know what you want, and I'll get you there. I promise."

And then he started to move, loving her slowly, deeply, endlessly. He kissed her lips, caressed her breasts, stroked her center. She gasped, she sighed and, finally, she came apart in his arms, shattering in unison with him.

Allison hadn't planned to fall asleep.

She didn't know that she had until she awakened in his arms. The glowing numbers of the clock on the bedside table revealed that it was 3:24. She breathed a sigh of relief, confident that Dylan, exhausted from all of the excitement of the previous day, would sleep for hours yet. But she should get back, so that he didn't wake up and find her bed empty.

She started to shift out of Nate's embrace, but his arms tightened around her.

"I have to go to my own room," she whispered in the darkness.

"Not yet." He rolled over on top of her. "I'm not done with you yet."

She felt the press of his erection against her belly, and the pulse of answering heat through her own veins. "So you're a morning person, are you?"

"Is it morning?"

She chuckled softly. "Or maybe you're just one of those guys who doesn't pay any attention to the clock when he's got a woman in his bed."

"Not a woman," he denied, brushing his lips to hers. "You."

They were simple words. Words that he'd probably spoken to countless women before her. But right now, with his body rising over and into her, she didn't care. Right now, she was the one in his bed, in his arms.

But even as her body responded to his touch, even as he drove her up and sent her flying over the edge, she held herself back from taking a bigger fall. Because she knew that if she gave him her whole heart, she would never get it back.

"Are you done with me now?" she asked, when she was finally able to gather enough breath to speak.

"Not even close," he said. "But I know you need to get back to your room before Dylan wakes up."

"I do." She brushed a soft kiss to his lips. "Thanks."

He didn't fall back to sleep right away.

After Allison left his bed, Nate couldn't stop thinking about the instinctive response he'd given when she'd asked if he was done with her.

Not even close.

It was true.

She was under his skin. She filled his thoughts when he was awake and haunted his dreams when he was asleep. He'd never been so preoccupied by a woman—any woman.

He wondered that an unexpected snowstorm could have had such an impact on his life, but everything had changed for him when he spent that night in St. Louis with Allison. Or maybe everything had changed at the Christmas party. He only wished he could be sure that she felt the same way.

He knew the fact that she'd spent the past few hours in his bed didn't magically alleviate all of her concerns about a relationship with him. And he couldn't blame her for that. She was wary of his reputation—a reputation he'd enjoyed building.

Unfortunately, he was now paying the price for it—having to convince the sexy single mom that he wasn't the careless and indiscriminate playboy he used to be. It wasn't going to be an easy task, but he wanted her not just to know that she could depend on him—but to actually do so.

When Allison finally returned to her room, she checked on Dylan, slipped into her pajamas, then fell face-first into her own bed.

She woke up several hours later to discover his was empty.

She wasn't surprised that he was up—a quick glance at the clock showed that it was almost 10:00 a.m. She couldn't remember the last time she'd slept so late—not that she'd gotten a lot of sleep. It had been almost five before she'd left Nate's room and returned to her own, at which time her son had been sleeping soundly.

But she was surprised that the room was quiet, making her wonder where Dylan might be and what he was doing. She wasn't really concerned. He wasn't the type of kid to wander too far on his own, especially in unfamiliar surroundings.

And then she noticed that the adjoining door was open.

Moving closer, she peeked through to see that Dylan was in Nate's sitting area, snuggled up in the middle of the sofa eating dry cereal out of a single-serve box from the mini-pantry. Nate was seated beside him and, judging from the sound emanating from the television, they were watching highlights of the qualifying that they'd both seen live the day before.

Looking at the two of them together, she felt a pang inside her chest to realize how much she wanted what Nathan was giving her son this weekend: a man who paid attention to him, who actually wanted to hang out with him.

Jeff had been a great dad in the beginning—attentive to

and doting on their baby. But his life was with Jodie now, his attention focused on their family. He still went through the motions with Dylan, because he was his son and his responsibility, and Jeff had always been big on responsibility. It was, after all, the reason he'd married her. He wasn't so big on warmth and affection.

She wouldn't have said Nate was, either, but he'd surprised her in so many little ways. Not just the trip, but the consideration he'd shown for her son's introverted personality. He'd given Dylan opportunities—so many wonderful and glorious opportunities—but he'd never pushed him beyond his comfort zone. He'd listened to what the boy wanted and had let him set the pace. He'd gone above and beyond for both of them this weekend, and seeing him with Dylan now, she was afraid her son was going to start to want more, expect more. And she knew that Nate wasn't a man who could give it.

Because a weekend away with a kid was one thing—being part of his life on a daily basis was another.

He'd been generous to a fault. Anything that Dylan expressed an interest in—T-shirts, pennants, posters—he bought for the boy. But far more than the merchandise, her son needed the time and attention that Nate gave him. She knew it didn't matter how much she made herself available to her little boy—he needed a man in his life on a more consistent basis. And if she wasn't careful, she might find herself dreaming about things that couldn't be.

"Are you guys going to lounge around here all day or are we going to go to the track?"

"The track!" Dylan voted.

"After a real breakfast," Nate suggested. "Man cannot live on dry cereal alone."

Dylan giggled, and Allison's heart swelled.

She couldn't remember the last time she'd heard such a

childish and carefree sound emanate from her son, and she knew that she would never forget this trip.

"Breakfast sounds good," she agreed.

"You going in your pajamas?" Nate asked.

Dylan giggled again.

She smiled. "Give me half an hour to shower and get dressed."

The rest of the weekend passed in a blur. Afterward, Allison was hard-pressed to recount a lot of specific details. She knew that Ren didn't take the checkered flag, but he came across the finish line in sixth place, which her son assured her was "an awesome run." She was pleased for the driver and the whole Garrett/Slater Racing team, but what made the strongest impression was the feeling of happiness that filled her heart to overflowing. And that happiness was the result of so many factors: the carefree sound of her son's laughter, the pure joy on his face, the slow emergence from his shell, the feeling of contentment when Nate linked his hand with hers and the giddy excitement of being naked in his arms.

And as they merged with the crowd exiting the stadium, Dylan's hands firmly clasped in each of hers and Nate's so that they didn't get separated, it occurred to her that they looked like a family—like so many other families around them. And the yearning sliced through her like a dagger.

She wanted to be part of a family again—not just for Dylan but for herself. But she knew that what they'd shared with Nate this weekend was only the illusion of family. It wasn't real and it wouldn't ever be real, and the longer she let herself cling to the fantasy, the more it was going to hurt when reality wrenched it out of her grasp.

It would be easier, although not painless, to let go before that happened. Which meant that when they got back to Charisma, she would take a step back, away from Nate. It was the only way to protect her son's heart—and her own.

She was so preoccupied with her own thoughts as they made their way to the car that it took her a while to notice that Dylan's breath was coming in short, shallow gasps. She'd been on high alert all weekend, worried that the excitement and the dust and fumes would trigger a flare-up of his asthma, but he'd been fine—until now. She pulled him out of the crowd and crouched down in front of him. She was conscious of Nate's presence behind her, but she kept her focus on her son. His face was pale and clammy and he coughed weakly.

"Relax," she said, tamping down the anxiety in her own belly to ensure that both her gaze and her voice were steady.

Dylan nodded, but she could read the familiar panic in his eyes.

Her hands were shaking as she opened her purse, locating both the bottle of water that she habitually carried and her son's emergency inhaler. She opened the water first and helped him take a few sips.

"Okay?"

He nodded again. She shook the medication, then removed the cover and passed the inhaler to him. Dylan closed his lips around the mouthpiece and pressed down on the pump.

"Breathe in," she reminded him. "Now hold."

She kept her attention focused on him, waited for his nod.

"Okay—one more," she suggested.

He did as she instructed, taking in a second dose of the medication.

"Is there anything I can do?" Nate asked.

She shook her head. "He's okay now."

Dylan still looked pale, but he was definitely breathing better and he wasn't making that wheezing sound that always made her blood run cold. She'd learned to cope with his asthma—both the daily regimen and the occasional flare-ups—but she still hated to see him suffer, hated even more knowing there was nothing she could really do to help.

He was clinging to her now, almost as if he might not be able to stand up on his own. She picked him up, thankful that he was on the small side for his age—barely four feet tall and not quite fifty pounds. But it wasn't going to be easy for her to carry him the rest of the way to the parking lot.

"Let me take him," Nate offered, obviously having come to the same conclusion.

She felt compelled to protest, because as great as he'd been with Dylan all weekend, her son seemed to prefer the comfort of his mom even over his dad when he was recovering from a flare-up. "Thanks, but—"

Nate didn't let her finish. He just lifted her son out of her arms and into his own. To her surprise, Dylan didn't protest. In fact, he curled an arm around Nate's neck, dropped his head onto his shoulder and closed his eyes.

The unhesitating display of trust and confidence worried her almost as much as her son's labored breathing.

It took them ten more minutes to make the trek to their rental car, another forty to get out of the parking lot, and thirty after that to the airport. The whole while that he was driving, Nate kept checking the rearview mirror to make sure Dylan was okay. His skin was still pale, and he suddenly looked not just younger than his nine years but fragile.

"Are you sure we shouldn't take him to the hospital?" he asked, as he took the turnoff to the airport.

"I'm sure."

"What if he has another attack while we're in the air?"

"He won't," she said. "But if he does, I have his inhaler, and if he did need to go to a hospital, I'd rather it was in Charisma where they have all of his medical records."

He nodded.

Anthony was waiting when they arrived. Having already

completed his preflight check, he announced that they were
cleared for takeoff. Dylan was asleep, his head snuggled
against his mother's side, almost before the wheels were
off the ground.

The asthma attack—or flare-up, as Allison insisted on
calling it—had freaked Nate out a little. He'd never seen anything like it before and he didn't think he wanted to again.
Listening to the kid struggle for breath, he'd felt useless and
helpless…and responsible.

"I'm sorry," he said to Allison now.

She seemed startled by the statement. "Why?"

"Because I didn't think about his asthma. When I made
the arrangements for the weekend, I never considered that
it would have a negative impact on his health."

"Don't be sorry," she said. "Because I'm not. And I guar-
antee you that Dylan isn't. In fact, I'm sure he would say
that this was 'the *best* weekend *ever*.'"

He managed to smile at that.

"The truth is he might have had a flare-up even if we'd
stayed at home this weekend."

"Now you're just trying to make me feel better."

"A little," she admitted. "But it's true. There are some
common triggers—cigarette smoke and dust are big ones
for Dylan, and he's more susceptible when he gets overex-
cited. And there are other times when his airways start to
close up for no apparent reason."

"How do you stay so calm and unruffled?"

"It's an act," she admitted. "Because I know that I have
to stay calm to keep him calm, but seeing him struggle for
breath terrifies me—every single time."

Nate shook his head, a wry smile on his face. "You're an
amazing mom, Alli."

"I try," she said. "And he makes it easy most of the time."

He hesitated for a moment. "Do you ever think about
having more kids?"

She sighed and leaned back in her seat, her hand softly ruffling her son's hair as he slept. "When Dylan was younger, I used to think that it would be nice for him to have a brother or a sister. Now he has two sisters and a brother on his dad's side—" she shrugged "—and that doesn't quite seem to be the big happy family that I always wanted for him."

"What about what *you* want?" he pressed.

She looked away. "I'm old enough to know that I can't always have what I want."

Which didn't really answer his question at all.

Dylan woke up when they landed in Raleigh, then fell asleep again in the car when Nate drove them home. But he was relieved to see that the kid's color was better and he was breathing more normally. And when he lifted Dylan out of the car to carry him up to his apartment, he snuggled against him, and somehow the weight of the little boy in his arms lifted his heart.

Allison pulled back the covers on Dylan's bed so that Nate could put him down. Then she stripped off his shoes and socks, eased him back onto his pillow and pulled the sheet up over him again.

"I guess I should let you crash, too," Nate said, as they tiptoed out of Dylan's room.

She nodded as she walked him to the door. "It was a fabulous weekend but a busy one, and I am exhausted."

So he kissed her goodbye—and wished that she would ask him to stay.

Chapter Thirteen

Monday night, just before dinner, Nate showed up at Allison's apartment with a bag of souvenirs that Dylan had forgotten in the backseat of his car.

"Thank you," Allison said. "Dylan was asking for it as soon as he woke up this morning."

"I should have given it to you at the office," he admitted. "But then I wouldn't have had an excuse to stop by and see him."

"You came to see Dylan?"

"Dylan *and* you," he clarified.

She stepped away from the door so that he could enter. "He's in his bedroom—doing his homework."

"Then he won't catch me stealing a kiss from his mom," Nate said, pulling her close.

She kissed him back, because any pretense of indifference would be nothing more than that. The truth was, she wanted him too much. She wanted him to come in the door at dinnertime every night, to share every meal with her and Dylan, to hang out with her son and sleep with her in her bed. But wanting a real relationship with Nathan was like wanting to hold running water in her hands.

"I think I deserve a lot of credit," he said, when he finally eased his mouth from hers.

"You are very good at that," she told him.

"I wasn't referring to the kiss but my restraint—I've been

wanting to do that all day, but I managed to hold back until now."

"I appreciate your restraint." Though she'd recently begun to accept that many of her coworkers knew she'd been spending a lot of time with her boss outside the office. In the staff room that morning, no fewer than half a dozen people had asked about her trip and, since her weekend plans weren't usually noteworthy, she could only assume that the curiosity was actually about her involvement with Nathan.

He rubbed his lips lightly against hers again. "It was worth the wait."

She stepped out of his arms when the timer sounded on the oven. "I suppose you want to stay for dinner."

"I wouldn't turn down an invitation."

At the racetrack, he'd been a generous and kind friend to Dylan. In the bedroom, he'd been a thoughtful and considerate lover. At the office, he was a demanding but fair employer. She recognized and accepted him in each of those roles. What worried her was that those roles were starting to overlap, and it was getting harder for her to keep their relationship compartmentalized.

Nathan Garrett doesn't do relationships.

It was more than water cooler talk—it was the truth. He was thirty-three years old, and while he was rarely without female companionship, he'd never been married or engaged or even—at least in the four years since he'd moved back to Charisma from New York—had a serious relationship. There had been speculation, when he was dating Mallory, that she might be the one to get him to make a commitment, but it hadn't happened. And when they went their separate ways, no one was really surprised.

He was, everyone said, a love 'em and leave 'em kind of guy. So why was he still hanging around? Why was he being so nice and kind and reliable? Why was he making her think that she could actually depend on him?

These questions plagued her all through dinner. Thankfully, he didn't seem to notice her preoccupation as he and Dylan kept up a steady stream of chatter, recounting their favorite moments from the weekend, speculating on Ren's chances in the next race. She didn't pay much attention to their conversation—not until Dylan mentioned wanting to see a race at Daytona and Nate casually responded that he'd see what he could do. She stood up abruptly and began clearing the table.

Nate offered to help, but she waved him off. She couldn't talk to him right now, because she knew that if she did, she wouldn't be able to hold back her feelings. She was furious with Nate for letting her son hope for something that wouldn't ever happen—and even more furious with herself for hoping it would.

Nate retreated to the living room to play video games with Dylan. Though her son tried to bargain for another half hour, she refused to be swayed. It was a school night and almost his bedtime already. With a disappointed sigh, he said goodnight to Nate—then impulsively wrapped his arms around him in a quick hug before he went to get ready for bed.

Nate, reading her mood, didn't stay. He thanked her for dinner and kissed her goodbye, then he was gone.

She should have been relieved. Instead, she felt confused and ungrateful and—dammit all—sorry that he'd gone. But she pushed those emotions aside and went to tuck Dylan into bed.

He was already snuggled under the covers, thumbing through the pages of the race program he'd brought home from the weekend at Bristol.

Dylan had been passionate about stock car racing long before he ever met Nathan. But before his birthday, it hadn't seemed so real—at least not to Allison. Now that he'd been to an actual race, he was completely obsessed with every aspect of the sport.

"Do you think I could be a crew chief someday?"

"I think you can be whatever you want to be," she told him, because she didn't ever want him to feel as if any dream was out of his reach. And because she was grateful he didn't want to drive the cars around a track at two hundred miles per hour.

He closed the cover of the program and set it aside. "Is Nate your boyfriend now?"

"We're friends," she acknowledged.

"Does he kiss you and stuff?"

Oh Lord—where were these questions coming from? How was she supposed to respond? And what was the "stuff" to which he—at nine years of age—was referring?

"We're friends," she said again. "And Mr. Garrett—Nate—is also my boss, so it wouldn't be a good idea for him to be my boyfriend."

"Why not?"

"Because it would be awkward for us to work together when he stopped being my boyfriend."

Dylan frowned at that. "Why would he stop being your boyfriend?"

"Because sometimes relationships don't work out the way we want them to."

"Like you and Dad," he guessed.

"Yes, like me and your dad," she confirmed.

"But now dad's got Jodie, so you should have someone, too."

"And maybe someday I will."

"Why can't Nate be that someone?" he persisted. "Don't you like him?"

"Yes, I like him," she admitted. *Probably too much.*

"I like him, too."

"I know you do." She pushed his hair away from his face and bent down to touch her lips to his forehead.

"I should have wished for Nate."

"What do you mean?"

"For my birthday—when I made a wish before blowing out the candles. I wished for a Ren D'Alesio jacket, because I didn't really know Nate then. But now I wish that I'd wished for him to be my new dad."

The wistful tone proved to her how much he wanted—needed—a steady and supportive male presence. She knew that Dylan loved his father and that Jefferson returned his affection, but her son needed more than a few hours on Wednesday and every other weekend. And it worried her to realize that he was looking to Nate for that more.

He'd been beyond great the whole time that they were in Tennessee, but that fantasy weekend bore little resemblance to the reality of her life and the daily responsibilities of caring for and raising a child. Nate couldn't have any idea about that because he didn't do commitment, he didn't do long-term, he didn't do relationships. Because she knew all of that, she trusted that she was smart enough not to fall for him.

But her son, basking in the attention of a man who listened to what he had to say and enjoyed spending time with him, didn't know that Nate wouldn't stick around. And she didn't know if she could protect him from the heartache that would follow.

She'd been carrying the letter marked "Personal and Confidential" in her purse for weeks, hoping that John would stop by the office so that she'd have an opportunity to give it to him. Two days after she got back from Tennessee, he finally did.

When he smiled, it was the same warm, familiar smile she'd seen on his face every day for six years. It was a kind face, an honest face and—since the heart attack he'd suffered over the holidays—a weary face.

After a brief meeting with the new CFO, he offered to take Allison for coffee.

"I'm glad you came in today," she said, when she took a seat across from him. "There's something I need to give you."

"What's that?"

She pulled the envelope marked 'Personal and Confidential' out of her purse and handed it to him.

"Oh." He stared at the handwriting on the front for a long minute but made no effort to open it.

"Several envelopes like this have crossed your desk over the years," John noted, "but you've never asked me about them."

"I assumed *Personal and Confidential* meant just that."

He smiled. "But you must have questions."

"Of course," she admitted. "I also know the answers are none of my business."

Truthfully, she didn't want to know the secrets he was alluding to. Though the distinctly feminine handwriting triggered certain suspicions, she wasn't anxious to have those suspicions confirmed.

John lifted his cup to his lips again. "Let's talk about something else," he suggested. "How are things with Nate?"

"He's settled in without any problem," she said.

Her former boss's smile was indulgent. "That's great but not what I was asking."

"Oh?"

"I might be old but I'm not blind, and I can see that there's something between the two of you."

She felt her cheeks flush and dropped her gaze to her cup. "It's not…really…anything."

"He's a good man, Alli. I used to worry about his reputation," John admitted to her now. "One of the reasons I kept putting off my retirement is that I wasn't sure Nate was ready for the responsibility of the corner office.

"I had no doubts about his ability to do the job, but I wondered whether he would be able to balance the professional responsibilities with his personal life. In the past two months, he's grown and matured more than I anticipated, and I suspect that has as much to do with you as the promotion.

"So when you say that whatever is between you and Nate isn't really anything, I hope you're wrong. For both of your sakes."

If his insight had unnerved her, this statement outright baffled her. "I can't imagine that the board would approve of a relationship between the CFO and his executive assistant," she protested.

"No one should have the right to approve or disapprove of a personal relationship between consenting adults," John insisted. "And I promise that no one is going to have any issue with a relationship that is obviously so right for both of you."

Allison appreciated the sentiment, but she wasn't sure she believed it. Especially when she was finishing up her lunch in the staff room later that day and Melanie Hedley took the empty seat beside her.

"I heard that you spent the weekend in Tennessee with Nathan."

Allison hadn't expected that their mutual absence from the office on Friday would go unnoticed, but she was unnerved to realize that news of their getaway had spread so quickly and widely. "My son is a racing fan," she explained. "We went to see the race, and Nate was there, as well."

Melanie unwrapped a prepackaged sandwich from the cafeteria. "Did you have a good time?"

"Yes." She kept her response concise, aware that any information she gave would only serve as grist for the rumor mill.

"I owe you an explanation."

"About what?"

"My trip to Vail over the holidays."

She shook her head. "You don't—"

"I didn't go *with* Nathan," Melanie forged ahead, ignoring Allison's protest. "Not in that sense, anyway. We went to a couple of the same parties and had lunch that one day, but that was it."

"Why are you telling me this?"

"Because I've seen the way he looks at you."

"How does he look at me?" The question slipped out before her brain could still her lips.

Melanie's sigh was wistful. "The way most women only hope a man will look at her."

Allison wanted to believe it was true. More, she wanted to believe it could last. But as much as she enjoyed being with Nathan—and she knew that Dylan did, too—she couldn't help but worry. Because she knew that the more deeply he got involved in their lives, the bigger the void would be when he wasn't there anymore. She had to be prepared for that time—and try to prepare her son for the same eventuality.

The weekend in Tennessee had been a success on a lot of levels. Nate had had the pleasure of rekindling his relationship with Allison, and he'd also gotten to know her son. So he didn't understand why she'd taken not just one but a dozen steps back since they'd returned to Charisma.

He knew that she still believed there were people at the office who were unaware of their personal relationship and, because it seemed important to her, he was playing along. But he was growing increasingly frustrated by her determination to keep him at a distance.

Since Monday, when he'd stopped by her apartment, he hadn't seen her outside the office. They'd talked, via text messages and telephone, but every time he suggested they get together, she turned him down. On Tuesday, she had to help Dylan study for a science test; on Wednesday, Dylan's usual night with his dad, she already had plans to go to a movie with Chelsea; on Thursday, she had to take Mrs. Hanson to the airport, because her elderly neighbor was going to Boston to visit her sister.

On Friday, after they'd finished finalizing his itinerary for an upcoming trip to San Diego, he told her that he was going to his cousin's house that night to help with some minor home repairs.

"But I shouldn't be too late," he said. "And I'd like to come by to see you and Dylan afterward."

"Actually, I was thinking that it might be good for Dylan and I to have some one-on-one time tonight."

Which might have made sense to him if he'd spent every other night of the week with them. But since he hadn't been to her apartment since Monday, the implication of her statement was obvious. "You don't want to see me?"

"I don't want him—or me," she admitted, "to start thinking that hanging out with you on a Friday night is the norm."

"You don't think I'm going to stick," he realized.

"Because you don't," she said gently.

And he couldn't blame her for believing that. Because it was true—or it had been in the past. But with Alli, everything was different. Or maybe it was only different for him.

"Neither of us made any promises—and I'm not asking for any," she continued in the same reasonable tone. "We both know what is and what isn't, but I don't know how to explain it to Dylan, and I don't want him to start thinking it's something that it isn't."

"Do we?" he challenged.

She frowned. "Do we what?"

"Do we both know what is and what isn't?"

"I thought so," she said, just a little warily.

He wanted to push for a more complete answer—to make her define their relationship. But he wasn't sure what he hoped she would say, and he was afraid that he didn't want to hear her answer.

He'd always been careful to ensure that the women he dated didn't have any expectations, so that he was free to walk away without remorse when the relationship was done.

Whether that was a few weeks or a few months, the one constant was that he walked away.

But he didn't want to walk away from Allison and Dylan—not today, not tomorrow and not any time in the foreseeable future. It was the only thing he knew for certain. As for the rest, he honestly didn't have a clue.

Lauryn looked more wary than happy to see Nate and Andrew when they showed up at her door Friday night. On their previous visit, she'd let them hang the shelves in the baby's room but had balked at their offer to help with other tasks. Because he anticipated continued resistance, and because Rachel was working late finishing up the flowers for a wedding the next day, Andrew brought his daughter along.

"This is a surprise," Lauryn said when she opened the door. And though she eyed her adult cousins warily, the little girl got a warm smile and a hug.

"Mommy and I made cookies," Maura told her "aunt," offering the tin she carried.

"What kind of cookies?"

"There's chocolate chip and peanut butter."

"Peanut butter are my favorite," Lauryn admitted.

"We could have some with a glass of milk—cookies are always better with milk," Maura told her.

"That sounds like a great idea," she said, opening the door wider so that they could enter. "But why do I think your dad and Uncle Nate aren't here for milk and cookies?"

"They came to fix your railing," Maura said.

"Did they?"

"Maura—why don't you take those cookies into the kitchen while Uncle Nate and I talk to Aunt Lauryn?" Andrew suggested.

"Okay," the little girl agreed readily.

"You didn't know we were coming?" Nate said to Lauryn.

"Since you didn't call to tell me—and I know I didn't call to ask—how would I know?"

"I saw Rob at the store yesterday," Andrew said, referring to Play On—the local sporting goods store owned by Lauryn's husband. "He said he didn't have the right tools to fix the railing and asked if I could give him a hand because he's worried about you going up and down to the laundry room without something to hold on to."

"Why were you at the store?" Lauryn asked suspiciously.

"Maura wants to play Little League this year so I took her in to get a baseball glove."

"Oh." She still looked skeptical, but Nate could tell that she wanted to believe her husband cared enough to at least express concern, even if he wasn't prepared to do anything about it.

"Go have your cookies with Maura," Nate suggested. "We know where the basement is."

"It smells a little musty down there," she warned. "We had a bit of a leak after all that rain last week."

"There's a sealer you can get for foundation cracks," Andrew told her.

She looked away as she nodded. "Rob said he was going to look into it."

Nate bit his tongue. Her husband had said a lot of things since he'd married her—unfortunately, he had proven time and again that he was all talk and no action.

When she'd gone, he followed his brother down the stairs. "It baffles me that she ever saw anything in him."

"But she obviously did, or she wouldn't have married him."

"And now they're going to have a baby." He knew he should be happy for his cousin, because he knew how much she wanted a family of her own. But he also suspected that she was hoping a child might somehow miraculously fix all of the problems in her marriage, and he didn't see that happening.

"And Lauryn's going to be a great mom." Andrew assessed the wall—shaking his head at the holes where the previous railing had been nailed into the drywall but not secured.

"I have no doubt about that," Nate agreed. "I'm just afraid she'll end up being a single mom."

His brother set his toolbox down on the step. "If she does, she'll handle it."

"I can't imagine it's easy to take care of a baby without any help."

"As if she'd ever be alone in this family."

Nate smiled wryly at that. "Good point."

"Which makes me think that there's someone other than Lauryn on your mind," Andrew noted.

"Alli," he admitted.

His brother's brows lifted. "I heard something about the two of you, but I assumed—based on the conversation we had a few months back—that it was unfounded gossip. Because I know you wouldn't be so foolish and shortsighted as to sleep with your secretary."

"It's not as if we're going at it on her desk," he said. But then, because he knew his older brother had always been a stickler for the rules, he couldn't resist adding, "At least not during business hours."

Andrew shook his head as he released the end of the measuring tape. "And what's going to happen when you decide you've had enough—how are you going to feel about working with her then?"

Because he didn't know—couldn't imagine—he only shrugged. "We'll figure it out."

"Isn't it past time for you to be doing that?"

"What do you mean?"

"You've been seeing her for—how long now?"

Nate shrugged again. "A few months, I guess. On and off."

"That must be a record for you."

"I dated Mallory for almost six months."

"She's a flight attendant who was out of the country more than she was in it during those six months," Andrew reminded him. "That wasn't a relationship—it was a series of one-night stands with the same woman."

He scowled, uncomfortable to realize that his brother's assessment of the relationship was entirely correct.

"But at least she didn't work for you," Andrew pointed out.

"That was one of the reasons Allison didn't want to get involved," Nate admitted. "Actually, she had a lot of reasons she didn't want to get involved."

"Including her son?" his brother guessed.

He nodded.

"I heard you took both of them to Bristol last weekend."

"I did," he confirmed.

"How did that go?"

"Better even than I hoped. Dylan had a great time. Of course, Daniel set us up with complete access, so he got to go inside the garage and tour the hauler and meet Ren and his pit crew."

Andrew sat back on his heels and studied his brother.

"What?" Nate asked warily.

"You've really fallen for her—for both of them."

He scowled. "Just because we had a good time together doesn't mean I'm looking for anything more than that."

"You're right," Andrew agreed. "It was probably a relief to get home at the end of the weekend and dump them off at their place."

"I didn't 'dump them off.'"

"But you must have been happy to get back to the peace and quiet of your own condo. Spending a whole weekend with a woman and her kid must have worn on your nerves."

"Dylan's a good kid."

"So why are you hanging out with me instead of them tonight?"

He shrugged. "Alli said that she wanted to spend some time alone with her son tonight."

"Hmm."

"What does that mean?"

"I guess I was just thinking that maybe her take on the weekend wasn't the same as yours."

"She had a great time."

"I'm sure she did," Andrew placated. "But sometimes spending that much time with one person changes the way you see them."

"What are you suggesting—that she's bored with me?"

"I know that's never happened to you before, but it is a possibility."

"Like hell it is."

Andrew actually laughed.

"I'm glad that you're amused."

"It is kind of funny," his brother insisted. "You've spent the better part of thirty-three years avoiding any kind of committed relationship and now you've finally fallen for a woman who might not want to commit to you."

"I haven't fallen for her," he said, though the denial sounded false even to his own ears.

"You don't think so?"

He wasn't sure what to think. He couldn't deny that he had strong feelings for Allison, but he wasn't ready to put a label on those feelings. "It's a long way from enjoying being with a woman to falling for her."

"It might be a long way, but it's a fast drop," Andrew warned.

"Are you actually going to use that drill or just hold on to it?"

"What's your hurry? It's not like you've got a hot date to rush off to."

The sound of the drill drowned out his pithy reply.

Chapter Fourteen

Allison snatched up the receiver before the first buzz of the intercom had finished sounding.

Even though she'd told Nate not to come, as soon as she'd settled Dylan into bed, she realized how foolish that request had been. He was right—she didn't want to count on him always being there. But while she was trying to protect her heart—and Dylan's—against the disappointment they would inevitably feel when Nate walked away, they were missing out on precious time that they could spend with him.

"Hey, Allison. It's me."

Anticipating Nate's voice, she was disappointed to hear her ex-husband's instead. "What are you doing here, Jeff?"

"I wanted to see you."

"Do you know what time it is?"

"Is it too late?"

"Yes, it's too late," she said, baffled that he even needed to ask the question. "I tucked Dylan into bed more than an hour ago."

"I didn't come to see Dylan."

She couldn't imagine any other reason that he would be there. "Then what are you doing here?"

"I needed someone to talk to."

"Did hell freeze over? Because I can't imagine any other condition under which I would be your first choice for conversation."

"Please, Allison. Let me come up. Just for a minute."

She glanced down at her flannel pajamas and fuzzy slippers, then decided she didn't care. "All right."

She waited at the door, so that he didn't have to knock, and immediately saw that he wasn't entirely steady on his feet.

"You've been drinking," she realized.

"I had a few."

She could smell the yeasty scent of beer on his breath from three feet away. "A few dozen?"

"I don't need you to nag me right now."

"And I don't need a drunk ex-husband at my door, so why don't I call you a cab and send you home to your current wife?" she suggested.

"Don't. Please."

It was the "please" that got to her. Jeff wasn't in the habit of asking for anything, and she wasn't good at saying no. She stepped away from the door so that he could come in. "Did you and Jodie have a fight?"

"Not exactly." He followed her into the kitchen and dropped into a chair while she measured out the grounds to make a pot of coffee.

"Then what—exactly?" she prompted.

"Jodie told me she was pregnant, and I walked out."

Aside from the fact that Jefferson the Fifth wasn't even a year old, she remembered Jeff telling her—after the birth of his second son—that Jodie would finally be satisfied that she now had the boy she always wanted. Apparently, three kids hadn't been enough, and Allison didn't know whether to offer her ex-husband congratulations or condolences.

"We weren't planning on having any more kids," he said. "In fact, I had a vasectomy six weeks ago."

"I'm guessing she's more than six weeks pregnant."

"According to the doctor's calculations, nine weeks and four days."

She handed him a mug of coffee—black—then poured another for herself, adding a splash of cream.

He lifted his cup to his lips when she sat down across from him. "I don't want another kid," he admitted. "And she knew I didn't want another kid."

"She didn't get pregnant on her own," she pointed out.

"She told me she couldn't get pregnant while she was nursing."

"That's a common misconception," she told him.

He seemed to consider that as he continued to sip his coffee. "Do you think she actually believed it?" he finally asked.

"I wouldn't want to speculate as to what she believed, but I know that you'll love this baby as much as you love all of your other kids."

"I'm not feeling so warm and fuzzy toward my wife right now."

"Every marriage has bumps in the road."

He stared into his cup. "Do you ever wonder if we gave up on ours too easily?"

She shook her head. "Our marriage was doomed from the start, because you were still in love with Jodie when you married me."

"I thought I was," he admitted. "But maybe I was wrong."

She got up to put her cup in the sink. He followed, stepping up behind her, trapping her between the counter and his body.

He was Dylan's father, and because of that, she felt a certain amount of affection toward him, a bond through the child they shared. That was why she put her hand on his chest, holding him at a distance instead of knocking him flat on his ass like he deserved.

"Don't do something you'll regret even more than the hangover you're going to have in the morning."

He covered her hand with his own. "We were always good together."

She moved away from him, into the living room, leaving him to stumble after her. "We had a few sparks that fizzled long before our marriage did."

He frowned at her dismissive summary of their shared past. "Are you still dating your boss? Is that why you're acting like this?"

"You can sleep on the sofa," she said, and retrieved a blanket from the chest-style coffee table.

"You didn't answer my question," he told her.

"Because my relationship with Nathan is none of your business."

"Either you're screwing the guy who signs your paychecks or you're not."

"Good night, Jefferson." She threw the blanket at him, then hit the light switch on her way out, plunging the room and him into darkness.

Nate thought about his conversation with Andrew for a long time after they left Lauryn's house that night. His brother seemed to have a knack for asking the hard questions—the ones that Nate had been avoiding for too long.

He cared for Allison—there was no denying that. And while he'd been unwilling to put a label on his feelings or quantify his affection for her, he knew it was safe to say that his feelings for her went deeper than anything he'd ever felt for another woman. But was that love?

She'd become an integral part of his life—and not just because he saw her every day at the office. She was the first person he thought of when he had good news to share, the last person he wanted to talk to before he went to sleep at night and the only person he could imagine sharing every part of his life for the rest of his life. And that was a scary realization for a man who had spent the better part of his thirty-three years carefully avoiding any discussion of the future or long-term with respect to his personal relationships.

He wasn't prone to melodrama, so he would never say that he couldn't live without her. But he didn't want to live without her. When he imagined his life without Allison and Dylan in it, it was empty and lonely.

The challenge now was going to be convincing Allison that his feelings for her were real.

It was almost too easy to picture a future for the three of them together. And it wasn't outside the realm of possibility to think that they might want to expand their family with another child or two someday. Not that he was in any hurry to have a baby with Allison—he wanted to spend time with her and Dylan first—but the prospect didn't completely terrify him. In fact, he kind of liked the idea.

No one had ever accused him of being particularly sensitive or insightful, but over the past few months he'd noticed something about Allison. Whenever they were out anywhere together and she saw a family—a man and a woman with a child or children—her attention would shift and her expression would grow wistful. He knew that she'd lost both of her parents when she was young, and he suspected that what she really wanted was a family—for her son and for herself.

He'd been fortunate to be raised by two parents who loved their children and each other. And while he was happy that both of his brothers had fallen in love and chosen to follow the path of holy matrimony, he hadn't been eager to do the same. His mother insisted he would change his mind when he met the right woman. His sister-in-law, Kenna, liked to tease that he was so accustomed to women falling all over him, he wouldn't recognize the right one if she hit him over the head with a two-by-four.

Nate had suspected that might be true—until he kissed Allison at the Christmas party. From that moment, he hadn't been able to get her out of his mind, and while it had taken him a while, he now knew that she was the woman he wanted for the rest of his life. Now he had to convince her of the same thing.

With only the first inkling of a plan sketched out in his mind, he stopped at the Morning Glory Café and picked up an assortment of muffins before heading to Alli's apartment.

She buzzed him up, but it was Dylan who met him at the door.

"Nate!" Dylan's shyness seemed to be a thing of the past, at least so far as Nate was concerned. And it tickled him to no end the way the kid's whole face lit up when he saw him. Or maybe it was the bakery box in his hand that was responsible for his obvious pleasure. "Doughnuts?"

Nate offered him the box. "I don't know how your mom feels about dessert for breakfast, but I don't know anyone who doesn't like doughnuts."

"I love doughnuts—'specially chocolate ones."

"I'm sure there're one or two chocolate ones in there."

"You didn't say anything about stopping by this morning," Allison said.

He watched as Dylan disappeared into the kitchen with his breakfast, then drew her into his arms. "I wanted to surprise you."

"Well, you succeeded."

He lowered his mouth to hers, kissed her long and slow and deep. "Good morning."

She smiled at him, that soft half smile that never failed to tug at his heart. "It is now."

And then a man walked into the room.

A man who, judging by his unshaven jaw and heavy-lidded eyes, had just woken up. He scrubbed a hand over his face. "What time is it?" he asked in a gravelly voice.

"Almost ten," Allison told him.

"Jodie's going to kill me."

"Probably," she acknowledged. "But I did call her last night, to let her know that you were here."

He nodded. "Thanks for that. And for letting me crash."

"Maybe you could say hello to your son before you head home," she suggested.

The "son" confirmed Nate's suspicions that the man was Jefferson Caldwell the Fourth.

"Is he up?" Dylan's father asked.

"In the kitchen."

He moved in that direction.

Nate watched him go, then turned to Allison, a little less confused now but more than a little livid. "What the hell is your ex-husband doing here?" he demanded.

"He slept on the sofa last night," she admitted.

"Why?"

"Because, only a few months after agreeing that they weren't going to have any more kids, he found out that his wife is pregnant with their fourth child."

"What does that have to do with you?"

"Nothing," she admitted. "But he was angry and upset and he went on a bit of a bender and ended up at my door—what was I supposed to do?"

"Pour him into a cab and send him home," Nate suggested.

"He's Dylan's father," she reminded him.

"And who am I?" he demanded. "What is my role in your life?"

She eyed him warily. "Why are you doing this? Why now?"

"Because I deserve to know where I stand with you. Because every time I think we've taken one step forward, you take two steps back. I wanted to see you last night," he reminded her. "But you wanted some space. And I gave it to you—only to find out that you spent the night with your ex-husband."

"You're completely misinterpreting the situation."

"Maybe I am," he admitted. "But sofa or not—I don't want you letting him sleep here again."

"I don't care what you want," she shot back. "I might have to take orders from you in the office, but that's where it begins and ends."

"I'm not giving you orders—I'm trying to set some parameters for our relationship."

"We don't have a relationship. We just sleep together on occasion."

He stared at her for a long minute. "Is that what you really think?"

"You've never given any indication of anything more than that."

"Then you haven't been paying attention, honey, because while you were sleeping with me, I was falling in love with you."

She took a step back, stunned.

"Yeah—it caught me off guard, too," he admitted. "I certainly never planned for this to happen, and I definitely never planned to tell you like that, but there it is. And now that you know how I feel, we can finally move forward."

"But…you don't do relationships."

"I didn't think so, either, but we've started to build a pretty good one—you, me and Dylan."

The inclusion of her son—without any hesitation—filled her heart to overflowing. But that was a purely emotional response, and she couldn't afford to let her heart rule her head. She needed to be logical—and she needed Nate to be logical, too.

"Or maybe you just want what both of your brothers have," she suggested. "And with me and Dylan, you get the whole package."

"If you really believe that, you're not giving either you or your son enough credit," he admonished. "I love you, Alli. What's between us is more than I expected—more than I ever thought I wanted. But now that I've found it, found you, you should know that I have no intention of letting you go."

She hadn't expected this, didn't know how to respond. Her head was spinning even as her heart was leaping for joy. She wanted to believe him, to let herself hope, but she didn't understand what had changed, why he apparently wanted something he'd never wanted before. And how could she know what she wanted when she'd never considered that a future with Nate was a possibility? "What about what I want?"

He smiled. "We both want the same thing—you just haven't realized it yet."

"You think you know my mind better than I do?"

"No, but I know your heart."

"I don't even know my heart," she protested.

"Yes, you do—you're just afraid to acknowledge what you're feeling."

Her chin lifted. "I'm not afraid."

"Good. Go get dressed and I'll give you a chance to prove it."

She should have asked where they were going. Ordinarily, she would have pressed for details, but the whole declaration-of-love thing had made her head spin so that she could barely form coherent thoughts. When he'd told her to get dressed, she went to get dressed because she needed some time to process what he'd said.

I was falling in love with you.

Could she believe it? Did she dare even let herself hope it might be true?

Jeff hadn't broken her heart, but he'd broken her trust. When they'd exchanged vows, she'd intended to honor them. She hadn't expected to fall madly in love and live happily ever after, but she'd thought that they both wanted the same thing: a family for their son. And she'd believed they were both invested enough in that dream to do everything in their power to make it happen. When her husband told her that he was still in love with Jodie, she hadn't been angry or even hurt so much as disappointed.

"Haven't you ever loved somebody so much you just couldn't imagine your life without him?"

"I guess I haven't," she admitted.

"Well, someday you will, and when you do, you'll understand why I can't be with you when I'm in love with someone else."

"But...what about Dylan?"

"He'll always be my son."

"But we were supposed to be his family. Forever."

And she'd wanted that for her son. And for herself. Losing both of her parents had left an enormous void in her life—a void she'd been desperate to fill. Marrying Jeff and having his baby had finally begun to do that, had given her the illusion that they were a family—at least for a while.

She hadn't been looking for the head-over-heels kind of love that he claimed to share with Jodie. She wasn't even sure she believed it existed. But now, with Nate, she thought she was finally beginning to understand.

She was so preoccupied with her own thoughts she didn't worry about where they were going. In fact, it wasn't until he pulled into the long driveway leading to an old farmhouse that had obviously been added on to and renovated numerous times that uneasiness settled in her belly like a ball of lead.

"Where are we?"

"My parents' house."

"Why are we here?" Dylan piped up from the backseat.

"Because I wanted you and your mom to meet my family," Nate told him.

The explanation seemed to satisfy Dylan, but it only raised more questions in Allison's mind. Because she, of course, had met his parents before. In fact, she'd met most of his extended family. But those introductions had occurred when she was behind a desk at Garrett Furniture or at a company event.

Which was one of the reasons she felt so awkward now. She hadn't wanted her relationship with Nate to become office gossip, though she'd been powerless to prevent it. And even so, she'd suffered no negative repercussions. In fact, most of her coworkers seemed not just to accept but approve of the relationship. But his parents were a whole other story—and she had no idea how they would react to the news that their son was involved with his executive assistant.

Jane Garrett was watering the planters on her front porch when Nate pulled into the driveway, but she set the can down on the step and came to greet them.

"This is a pleasant surprise," she said, sounding more pleased than surprised.

"You remember Allison Caldwell, Mom?"

"Of course," she said, smiling at Allison. "It's wonderful to see you again."

"And this is her son, Dylan," Nate said.

"It's a pleasure to meet you, Dylan."

He looked hesitantly at his mom. "Thank you?"

"Your dad's around back with Maura," Jane said. "Why don't we go join them?"

They found David Garrett playing catch with his granddaughter.

"Spring training," he explained, waving to them from a distance. "Maura has decided she wants to play the hot corner this season, so she's got to work on making the throw from third to first."

Dylan watched them, undisguised yearning on his face.

"Do you want to play?" Jane asked him.

"I don't have a glove."

"We have a whole box of gloves in the garage," she told him. "Why don't you let Nate show you where they are so you can find one that fits?"

Allison expected him to refuse, to want to stay with his mom more than he wanted to play catch.

But when Nate said, "Come on," her son willingly fell into step behind him.

She watched them walk away, worried that Dylan was already so attached to Nate, he was willing to follow wherever he led.

"Can I get you something to drink?" Jane asked. "We've got lemonade and sweet tea, and I'll put a pot of coffee on, because I'm sure that's what Nate'll want."

"Coffee sounds good," Allison agreed.

She followed Nate's mom into the house.

"What did my son do to put that worried look on your face?" Jane asked, as she set the coffeemaker to brew.

"I really shouldn't play poker, should I?"

The older woman chuckled. "No, you definitely should not."

"I think I'm more confused than worried," Allison admitted.

"Men do have a way of muddling up the simplest things," Jane said. "Maybe I can help you figure it out?"

She had to smile at the woman's not-so-subtle prying. "I'm not sure I'd even know where to begin," she hedged.

Jane got out a sugar bowl and matching pitcher, which she filled with cream, then set both on a serving tray.

"I don't know what Nate has told you," Allison said hesitantly.

"He hasn't told me anything," Jane admitted, adding mugs to the tray. "But the fact that he brought you and your son here says it all for him."

"You might be making a bigger deal out of this than it is," Allison said, a warning to Nate's mother as much as herself.

"Falling in love is scary," Jane said. "Opening up your heart to someone else is always a risk. I'd say that falling in love with a Garrett goes beyond scary to downright terrifying, because none of them do anything by half measures.

"They demand one hundred percent—but they give one hundred percent, too. I'd almost abandoned hope that Nathan would find a woman he could love completely and forever, but I'm glad to see that he didn't." The coffee had finished brewing, and she added the carafe to the tray. "The only question unanswered is whether you can love him the same way."

Chapter Fifteen

They stayed for lunch, because Jane insisted. And Jane and David were both so natural and easygoing, it wasn't nearly as awkward as Allison had feared it might be. But she was still relieved when the meal was over and it was time to go, because she needed to think about Jane's question—and she needed to be sure that her answer wouldn't be unduly influenced by the presence of Nathan's wonderful family. Dylan, on the other hand, was obviously reluctant to leave and he held tight to Nathan's mom when he said goodbye.

Dylan had grandparents—Jeff's mom and dad—but he didn't see them very often and they'd never been overly affectionate with their eldest grandson. By contrast, David Garrett had talked to him like an equal, and he'd listened to what Dylan had to say. Not that he said much—after all, he'd only met the man a few hours earlier—but he did talk a little bit about baseball and stock car racing and what kind of condiments made the best burgers. And Jane Garrett had made no secret of the fact that she adored him from the get-go. She offered him food and drink and, after the burgers were gone, homemade chocolate chip cookies.

Then, as they were leaving, Jane had hugged Allison, too. It had been a long time since Allison had known the comfort of a maternal embrace, and although she didn't cling, as her son had done, she wanted to. She wanted to be part of Nate's warm and wonderful family, and it was exactly that wanting that she knew could be dangerous.

* * *

When they got back to the apartment, Allison gave her son permission to play video games because she didn't want him overhearing the conversation that she needed to have with Nathan.

When the sound from the living room confirmed that Dylan's attention was otherwise engaged, Nate said, "Are you going to tell me what I did wrong?"

"I can't believe you even have to ask."

"Was spending a few hours with my parents so horrible?"

"It wasn't horrible at all," she admitted. "Your parents are wonderful people."

"I'm glad you think so," he said. "Because they said the same thing about you and Dylan."

"I just feel like I was…ambushed."

"How do you figure?"

"Because you had to know that taking me—and my son—to meet your parents would make them speculate about our relationship."

"What I know," he told her, "is that it's traditional for a man to take the woman he wants to marry home to meet his parents."

"Ohmygod." She sat down, hard, because her legs were about to go out from under her.

"Was that a good or a bad 'ohmygod'?"

"I don't know."

"It's true," he said. "I want to be your husband and Dylan's stepfather. I want a life with both of you."

She swallowed. "And when did you come to this realization?"

"Last night. About two minutes after I figured out that I loved you. And I do—I love you, Alli."

Those simple words, sincerely spoken, made her heart stutter. She couldn't battle against him and her own desires, but she was still afraid to admit how much she wanted everything he was offering.

"I've never said those words to another woman," he admitted.

"And that's another point."

"What's another point?"

"You've dated half the female population in this town—"

"I'm not going to apologize for the fact that there were other women before you."

"I'm not asking for an apology," she told him.

He looked frustrated. "You just want to keep throwing them up in my face."

"I just don't understand why you think you want a future with me when you've never even had a long-term relationship before."

"I'd say the obvious and simplest explanation is that none of those other women was you."

She blew out a breath as her heart stuttered again. "It scares me," she admitted, "that you always seem to know just what to say to make me want to believe you."

"I love you, Alli. I've never said those words to another woman because I've never felt this way before, and if you believe nothing else, please believe that."

"I don't know what I'm feeling," she admitted. "I've tried so hard not to fall for you, because I was sure that if I did, you'd break my heart."

He took her hands. "I promise, if you give me your heart, I will only cherish and protect it—for now and forever."

She wanted to believe him. She wasn't sure she'd ever wanted anything more than she wanted to believe him. But he was Nathan Garrett—perennial playboy. How could she trust what he was saying? How could she trust that what he wanted today would still be what he wanted tomorrow?

But wasn't not knowing the very definition of trust? Could she give him the benefit of the doubt? Take a leap of faith? She wanted to—but there was more than her own heart at risk. She had to think of her son, whose heart was so much more vulnerable and fragile than her own.

He'd been so young when his parents separated that he had no memories—good or bad—of their time together. But he was already attached to Nate, and she worried that if things didn't work out for them, her son would be devastated.

But what if things did *work out?*

Then Dylan would finally have the full-time family she'd always wanted for him—and for herself.

Nate could tell that her resistance was weakening. Her eyes, always so expressive, swirled with emotion.

"It doesn't make any sense to me," she admitted. "How can you go from casual to committed in the blink of an eye?"

"It wasn't in the blink of an eye," he denied. "And my feelings were never as casual as you apparently believed."

She nibbled on her lower lip.

"I don't know why it's you—I only know that it is. You're *it* for me. You and Dylan. I want to share my life with you, build a family together. I want to be with you—both of you—today, tomorrow and always.

"I…"

Whatever she'd intended to say was cut off by Dylan's entrance into the kitchen. Apparently he'd grown bored with video games, as he now carried the glove and ball that David Garrett had let him bring home.

"Can we go to the park?" he asked hopefully.

"Can you give us a few more minutes, buddy?" Nate asked. "Your mom and I are in the middle of something."

Allison shook her head. "No—go to the park. Please. I need some time alone to think about this."

"*We* need to talk about it," he insisted, reluctant to leave her alone with her thoughts when he knew she would think of all kinds of reasons to back away from him again.

"I can't talk about it right now," she told him.

So he walked over to the park with Dylan, confident that the boy, at least, was in his corner.

He knew he'd caught Allison off guard when he told her he loved her, and he hadn't expected a reciprocal declaration—although he'd hoped. After all, it was the first time he'd ever said the words to a woman, and it would have been nice to hear her confirm that she felt the same way.

And he was pretty sure that she did. When he touched her, when he kissed her, she couldn't hide her feelings for him. But apparently she wasn't yet ready to admit them, either.

So he decided that he could give her time, but he wasn't going to give up.

"Are you and my mom fighting?" Dylan's tentative question pulled him out of his reverie.

"Did it sound like we were fighting?"

The boy shrugged. "She sounded like she sounds when she's trying not to yell at me."

"Your mom's a little annoyed with me," he admitted.

There weren't many people in the park today—a couple of kids flying kites, a teenager walking a dog, a mom with a baby in a stroller, an older couple down by the pond, feeding pieces of bread to the ducks.

"Are you gonna marry her?"

"Where did you hear that?" he asked cautiously.

"Maura told me she's never met anyone you dated before, so it probably means you're gonna marry my mom."

"That's the plan," he admitted. "If I can get her to go along with it."

Dylan sighed. "Good luck with that."

"You don't think I can persuade her?"

"Did she say 'we'll see'? 'Cause if she said 'we'll see,' she meant 'no.'"

Nate smiled at that. "She said she needed some time to think about it."

"That doesn't sound very promising," the boy warned.

"Well, I'm not going to give up."

"How come?"

"Because when you love someone, you don't walk away."

"You love my mom?"

"Yeah," he said. "And I happen to think her son's pretty terrific, too."

"Her…oh, me," Dylan realized, and offered a shy smile.

Nate tapped the brim of the boy's baseball cap. "I know it's been just you and your mom for a long time. Are you okay with the idea of a stepdad?"

The boy hesitated, and Nate's breath backed up in his lungs as he waited for a reply. It occurred to him then that he might have assumed too much—not just about Allison's feelings but Dylan's. After all, the boy already had a father—it was possible that he had no interest in what Nate was offering. It was possible that neither Allison nor her son needed him as much as he'd realized he needed them.

Dylan looked up at him. "I think so," he finally responded in a solemn tone. "If it was you."

And Nate's breath whooshed out of his lungs. "Okay, then," he said, striving to keep his tone light. "Let's play ball."

When the intercom buzzed only a few minutes after Nate and Dylan had gone, Allison assumed they'd forgotten something. When she realized it was Chelsea in the lobby, she was only too happy for her friend's company.

"Look what I found at the flea market." She held up a *Racing World* magazine with Ren D'Alesio on the cover. "It's near mint condition, from his rookie season, when he was still with Team D'Alesio."

"That's…great."

Chelsea rolled her eyes at the lackluster response. "Dylan will love it."

"I'm sure he will," she agreed. "But he's at the park with Nate right now."

At home in Allison's apartment, Chelsea went to the fridge and found a pitcher of sweet tea, poured herself a glass. "I thought you weren't going to see him this weekend."

"Apparently he had a different idea."

"Do you want a glass of this—" Chelsea held up the pitcher "—or do you need something stronger?"

Allison shook her head. "I'm fine." Then she sighed. "No, I'm not fine. But I'm not thirsty."

"What happened?"

"He took me and Dylan to his parents' house today."

"Oh. Wow. That's a pretty big step."

"A leap," Allison agreed. "But that's not even the biggest one."

"So tell me."

"Apparently he had some time to think last night, and he realized that he loves me and Dylan and wants to marry me so that the three of us can be a family."

Her friend's eyes got misty. "That is so…perfect."

"I didn't say yes."

Chelsea narrowed her gaze. "You better not have said no."

"I didn't know what to say. I've been so busy telling myself that this wasn't—couldn't be—a real relationship, that I didn't see it coming. How could I?"

"Honey, even I could see that he was heading in this direction."

"Another man—maybe," Allison allowed. "But this is Nathan Garrett—the guy who's never committed to a future any farther away than breakfast the morning after."

"Because he was waiting for the right woman," Chelsea told her.

"And what if I'm not the right woman?"

"He seems to think you are."

"How can he know when he has no experience with relationships?"

"Would you feel better if he had a failed marriage—or at least a broken engagement—in his past?"

"Maybe," she admitted.

"Do you know how crazy that sounds?"

She nodded.

"Which is usually a sure sign that you're head over heels crazy in love," Chelsea warned.

"I've never been all the way in love before," she confided.

"I know."

"He could break my heart."

"That's always a risk," her friend agreed. "But I don't think he will. I think he's the man who can finally give you the family you've always wanted, be the dad that Dylan deserves and the man who makes you happy for the rest of your life."

"When did you join the Nate Garrett fan club?"

"When I saw the sparkle come back into your eyes."

Allison pouted. "I thought you'd be on my side."

"I am. Always. But I'm sorry if I can't sympathize with the fact that there's a gorgeous, sexy, charming and very rich man who wants to be part of your life and had the audacity to take you to meet his parents and mention the possibility of marriage."

"Are you trying to make me feel ridiculous?"

"Is it working?"

"Yes," she admitted.

Chelsea grinned. "Good."

The ball diamond was empty, so they took up positions on the infield and began to toss the ball back and forth.

Dylan had a great arm, but he needed to work on his catching. He often closed his hand before the ball was in the pocket, which meant that the ball bounced off the glove and rolled away. But the kid had potential, and Nate thought it would be fun to work with him—maybe even coach him in Little League someday.

After about fifteen minutes, Nate noticed that Dylan was slowing down—hesitating before he threw the ball back and not rushing to retrieve it when he missed.

"You getting bored?" Nate asked him.

Dylan shook his head. But when he bent down to pick up the ball, he started to cough. And instead of throwing it back, he clutched it against his chest.

Something about his posture set off warning bells in Nate's mind. He jogged toward the boy, heard the wheezing as he expelled air from his lungs, his breathing obviously labored. He immediately recalled the flare-up he'd witnessed when they were leaving Bristol. But Allison had been there then, not just to recognize the signs but to help administer the medication.

Nate dropped to his knees beside the boy and tried to remember what she'd done. He picked him up and carried him to the player's bench, sitting him down and urging him to keep his back straight and take slow, deep breaths in through his nose.

"Do you have your inhaler?"

The boy nodded again and reached into his pocket, and Nate exhaled a shuddery sigh of relief. He took the device from Dylan and shook it vigorously, as he remembered seeing Allison do.

"It's okay, buddy. Just relax and get some of this medication into your lungs."

He knew that the panic that went hand in hand with an attack inevitably made the situation worse, so he tried to keep his voice level so the boy wouldn't realize how close Nate was to panicking himself.

Dylan put the inhaler in his mouth, pushed down on the

pump and drew in a slow, deep breath. Then he coughed again and shook his head.

"What's wrong?"

He tried the pump again, then tossed the inhaler aside.

"Emp-ty," he said, as a single tear slid down his cheek.

Empty?

It was the perfect word to describe the hollow feeling in Nate's chest. He already had his phone in his hand, intending to call Allison.

He dialed 9-1-1 instead.

Allison was grateful that Chelsea was still with her when Nate called.

Since he'd only gone across the street to the park with Dylan, she immediately knew that something was wrong.

"What happened?"

"Dylan had an asthma attack."

"Bad?"

"I don't know," he admitted. "We're at Mercy—"

"I'm on my way."

She didn't protest when her friend took the keys out of her shaking fingers. They'd made this trip several times before, although the last time had been more than a year earlier.

"Don't let him see how worried you are," Chelsea reminded Allison as they walked through the ER doors together.

"I know."

"And try not to jump all over Nate before he has a chance to tell you what happened."

"What happened is that I let them go to the park without me. No—I didn't just let them, I practically shoved them out the door. I was so preoccupied, I didn't think—"

"You can't be with Dylan every minute of every day," Chelsea interjected gently.

"I should have been there," she insisted.

"Nate was there."

"Nate's not his father."

"You're right." It was Nathan himself who responded to her statement. "I have no legal connection to Dylan or you—but I love him anyway, and I'm going crazy because none of the doctors or nurses will tell me anything because I'm not family. So maybe you can get some information from them."

She refused to feel guilty for speaking the truth, for putting that wounded look on his face. And while she did intend to talk to the doctor, she wanted some information from Nate first.

"Why didn't he use his rescue inhaler?" she asked him.

"He tried. I think it was empty."

"Empty?" Her eyes filled with tears. "Dammit, Nate."

"I didn't know," he said. "I'm so sorry, Alli."

She just shook her head. "Where is he?"

"They took him into an exam room—"

She pushed past him and rushed toward the nurses' desk, with Chelsea on her heels.

Allison's best friend had always seemed a little guarded around him, so Nate was surprised when Chelsea came out to the waiting room and sat down beside him.

"Alli's in mama bear mode right now," Chelsea said. "Don't take anything she says personally."

He nodded, but he knew that everything her friend had said was true. He'd been irresponsible. Allison had trusted him with her son, and now Dylan was in the hospital.

"It was an asthma attack—and hardly his first one."

"I thought—" He looked away but he didn't dare close his eyes, because every time he did, he saw the fear and panic on the little boy's face as he fought to draw air into his lungs. "I was terrified—I didn't know what I was going to do if the ambulance didn't get there on time."

"It is terrifying, especially the first time, because there's nothing really you can do. If the inhaler doesn't work or if he doesn't have it—and yes, I was with him once when that happened—the next step is to seek medical attention."

"Have you been through this more than once with him?"

"So many times I lost count," she admitted.

"I can't imagine."

"You aren't responsible for what happened."

"While I appreciate the sentiment, I'm not sure I agree. And it's obvious that Alli doesn't."

"It's hard for a parent to be rational when their child is hurting."

He just nodded.

"He's going to be fine," Chelsea said. "He's been given a reliever medication as well as an oral steroid and is already responding to treatment. Dr. Roberts said his heart rate and blood pressure are good, and his breathing is improving."

He nodded again.

She stretched her legs out in front of her and crossed her feet at the ankles, obviously settling in for a long wait. "Do you have a ring?"

The abrupt change of topic caught him off guard. "What?"

"If you expect Allison to take your proposal seriously, you need a ring. Otherwise it seems like an impulse—and one she might think you'll later regret."

"I don't have a ring yet," he admitted. "I was planning to take Dylan with me to pick one out, so that he knows he's a part of it, too."

"Oh." Chelsea's eyes filled with tears. "That's good. She'll love that."

Nate could only hope that she was right.

While Nate was talking to Chelsea, Allison was on the phone with her ex-husband.

She knew their son was going to be fine, but she also knew that if the incident had happened when Dylan was in his father's care, she'd want to know about it. Of course, Jeff was a veteran of ER visits, so he asked all the usual questions and she reassured him that Dylan was okay—and now that she'd seen her son, she was willing to believe it. Jeff opted not to make the trip to the hospital but promised that he would stop by to see Dylan the next day.

After she hung up with Jeff, she went to find Chelsea, surprised to find Nathan was still in the waiting room, too.

Nate's not his father.

The words she'd practically snapped out at her friend echoed in the back of her mind. Maybe she'd spoken the truth, but her tone had been angry and accusatory, and though she hadn't intended to hurt Nathan, she couldn't deny that had been the result. Another truth was that Nathan had given her son more time and attention over the past month than the man who'd contributed to his DNA. Even now, even after the way she'd treated him, even while Jeff was at home with his new family, Nate was still there, pacing the waiting room and worrying about her son.

He can be the dad that Dylan deserves.

As Chelsea's words echoed in the back of her mind, Allison realized that he already was. In so many ways, he'd proven not only that he was capable of making a commitment, but he'd done so. She'd just refused to see it.

She'd been on her own for so long with Dylan, so accustomed to doing things on her own, that she wasn't sure she knew how to share her life. But she wanted to share it with Nate, if that was what he still wanted, too.

Chelsea spotted her first. "Any update?"

"Everything's good. Dr. Roberts just wants to keep an eye on him for another hour or so to make sure, but he figures we can go home after that."

"That's great," Chelsea said. "I'm just going to go in to say goodbye to him before I head home to get ready for work."

"You don't have your car," Allison said.

"I'll catch a cab."

Her friend kissed her cheek and walked out, leaving Allison alone with Nate. Well, alone with Nate and the half dozen other people who were waiting for medical attention.

"Do you want to see him?" she finally asked.

He nodded.

She turned and led the way, pulling back the curtain of an exam cubicle where Dylan was asleep on the bed. Nate hovered just inside the curtain, looking worried.

"He's fine," Allison assured him. "These episodes just wear him out."

She sat on a hard plastic chair beside the bed and reached for Dylan's hand. His eyelids flickered but didn't open. Nate took the chair on the other side of her.

"I owe you an apology," she said quietly.

"No, you don't," he denied.

But she nodded. "I blamed you because it was easier than accepting my own responsibility for what happened. I *never* let Dylan go anywhere without making sure that he has his inhaler with him. But I was distracted and confused—"

"That was my fault, too."

She shook her head. "None of this is your fault. You called 9-1-1. You kept him calm until the ambulance got there. You stayed with him, so that he wasn't alone."

"He wouldn't have needed the ambulance if I'd made sure he had a working inhaler before we left the apartment."

"Next time you will."

He looked at her hopefully. "You're going to let there be a next time?"

She managed a wry smile. "If all of the drama hasn't completely scared you off."

"I was terrified," he admitted. "But I'm not going anywhere. Like I told Dylan earlier—when you love someone, you don't walk away." He took her free hand, linked their fingers together. "And I'm not walking away from either of you."

She looked at their joined hands for a long minute, grateful not just for his support and his strength but for everything he'd added to her life just by being part of it. "I'm glad, because I love you, too," she finally admitted.

"Enough to marry me?"

Her eyes filled with tears. "Are you really proposing to me in a hospital cubicle?"

"I know you deserve candlelight and flowers. And a ring—Chelsea told me that I should have a ring. But I don't want to wait any longer." He released her hand and dropped to one knee beside her chair. "Allison Caldwell, will you marry me?"

"The where and the how don't matter," she assured him. "Only the who—and since you're the man I love, I want to say yes, but I need to talk to Dylan about this first."

"Say yes," Dylan said.

She turned to see that her son was now wide awake and grinning. "Don't you think we should talk about this?"

"Nah. Nate and I already talked—it's good."

He said it so simply, and with so much confidence, she knew it *was* good. And that it was going to get even better.

"Still on my knee here," Nathan reminded her. "Waiting for an answer."

"The answer is yes," she told him. "Definitely yes."

He stood up and lifted her into his arms, holding her tight, as if he wasn't ever going to let her go.

"I guess our relationship won't be a secret at work now," she noted.

He chuckled. "You're the only one who ever thought it was."

"Since it's not, do I get a ring?"

"As long as I get you and Dylan, you can have whatever you want."

"You." She touched her lips to his. "I want you."

"You've got me," he promised. "For now and forever."

* * * * *

Look for Ryan Garrett's story,
A FOREVER KIND OF FAMILY
the next installment in award-winning author
Brenda Harlen's miniseries for Harlequin Special Edition,
THOSE ENGAGING GARRETTS!
On sale May 2015, wherever Harlequin books are sold.

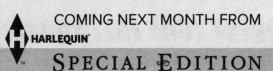

REQUEST YOUR FREE BOOKS!
2 FREE NOVELS PLUS 2 FREE GIFTS!

Ⓗ HARLEQUIN®

SPECIAL EDITION
Life, Love & Family

HSEI3R

***

Matteo knew he should be leaving—and had most likely already overstayed—but he found himself wanting to linger just a few more seconds in her company.

"I just wanted to tell you one more time that I had a very nice time tonight," he told Rachel.

She surprised him—and herself when she came right down to it—by saying, "Show me."

Matteo looked at her, confusion in his eyes. Had he heard wrong? And what did she mean by that, anyway?

"What?"

"Show me," Rachel repeated.

"How?" he asked, not exactly sure he understood what she was getting at.

Her mouth curved, underscoring the amusement that was already evident in her eyes.

"Oh, I think you can figure it out, Mendoza," she told him. Then, since he appeared somewhat hesitant to put an actual meaning to her words, she sighed loudly, took hold of his button-down shirt and abruptly pulled him to her.

Matteo looked more than a little surprised at this display of proactive behavior on her part. She really was a firecracker, he thought.

The next moment, there was no room for looks of surprise or any other kind of expressions for that matter. It was hard to make out a person's features if their face was flush against another's, the way Rachel's was against his.

If the first kiss between them during the picnic was sweet, this kiss was nothing if not flaming hot. So much so that Matteo was almost certain that he was going to go up in smoke any second now.

The thing of it was he didn't care. As long as it happened while he was kissing Rachel, nothing else mattered.

***

Don't miss MENDOZA'S SECRET FORTUNE
by USA TODAY bestselling
author Marie Ferrarella,
the third book in
THE FORTUNES OF TEXAS: COWBOY COUNTRY
continuity!

Available March 2015, wherever
Harlequin® Special Edition books and ebooks are sold.

JUST CAN'T GET ENOUGH
ROMANCE
Looking for more?

Harlequin has everything from contemporary, passionate and heartwarming to suspenseful and inspirational stories.

Whatever your mood,
we have a romance just for you!

Connect with us to find your next great read, special offers and more.

Facebook.com/HarlequinBooks

Twitter.com/HarlequinBooks

HarlequinBlog.com

Harlequin.com/Newsletters

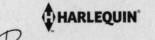

ⒽHARLEQUIN®

A *Romance* FOR EVERY MOOD™

www.Harlequin.com